"You!" Lissie pointed her finger at Menno. "What are you doing here?"

"Endie!" her son squealed and pulled away from Lissie.

"Jonah!" Naomi took off after her brother as he ran to the wagon to meet the great-aunt he'd heard so much about.

Lissie stared at Menno. For an instant, his face was one of pain and bewilderment. Then he smiled—the most handsome smile she had ever known.

"It's so good to see you. I'm here to pick you up and bring you home." As he spoke, he secured the wagon's brake and reins.

Lissie took another unsteady step back as he leaped down from the wagon.

"Eunice doesn't like driving such a distance, so she asked me to—"

"*Nay*," Lissie interrupted, so angry that tears filled her eyes. "You are not supposed to be *here*!" She glanced up at her aunt, intending to demand why she would betray her this way, but she was busy greeting Jonah.

Lissie returned her gaze to Menno. "I don't want you here. I didn't ever want to see you again."

Emma Miller lives quietly in her old farmhouse in rural Delaware. Fortunate enough to have been born into a family of strong faith, she grew up on a dairy farm, surrounded by loving parents, siblings, grandparents, aunts, uncles and cousins. Emma was educated in local schools and once taught in an Amish schoolhouse. When she's not caring for her large family, reading and writing are her favorite pastimes.

Books by Emma Miller

Love Inspired

Seven Amish Sisters

Her Surprise Christmas Courtship
Falling for the Amish Bad Boy
The Teacher's Christmas Secret
An Unconventional Amish Pair
Her Forbidden Christmas Match
The Widower Takes a Wife

The Amish Spinster's Courtship
The Christmas Courtship
A Summer Amish Courtship
An Amish Holiday Courtship
Courting His Amish Wife
Their Secret Courtship

Delaware Amish Brothers

Courting the Amish Widow

Visit the Author Profile page at LoveInspired.com for more titles.

COURTING THE AMISH WIDOW

EMMA MILLER

LOVE INSPIRED
INSPIRATIONAL ROMANCE

MIX
Paper | Supporting responsible forestry
FSC® C021394

LOVE INSPIRED®
INSPIRATIONAL ROMANCE

Recycling programs for this product may not exist in your area.

ISBN-13: 978-1-335-62155-9

Courting the Amish Widow

For questions and comments about the quality of this book, please contact us at CustomerService@Harlequin.com.

® is a trademark of Harlequin Enterprises ULC.

Love Inspired
22 Adelaide St. West, 41st Floor
Toronto, Ontario M5H 4E3, Canada
www.LoveInspired.com

HarperCollins Publishers
Macken House, 39/40 Mayor Street Upper,
Dublin 1, D01 C9W8, Ireland
www.HarperCollins.com

Printed in Lithuania

Because strait is the gate, and narrow is the way,
which leadeth unto life, and few there be that find it.
—*Matthew* 7:14

Chapter One

Kent County, Delaware
May

Menno Bontrager tightened and loosened the leather reins rhythmically as his wagon rolled down the country road at a steady pace. As he passed a field of newly sprouted corn, he tried not to dwell too much on how many years he'd been waiting for this day. All in *Gott*'s time, he reminded himself. They were halfway to town and would reach the bus stop before the love of his life, Lissie, arrived.

"No need to be nervous." His neighbor, Eunice Stutz, placed her blue-veined, wrinkled hand on his arm. She looked at him with gray eyes from behind round, wire-frame glasses. She'd be eighty-three soon, but she was still sharp-minded and able-bodied, a woman who didn't hesitate to tell a man what she was thinking.

"I'm not nervous," he said.

Eunice snorted.

"You look as nervy as a boy giving a girl a ride home from a singing for the first time," his grandmother, Sheba, chided, leaning forward on the buckboard seat to look at him.

Menno hadn't intended to bring his grandmother along,

too. Eunice was the one who had hatched this plan—him taking her to the bus stop with him to *help break the ice*, as Englishers liked to say. But then his grandmother, Eunice's best friend, insisted she go along, too.

"No reason to be nervous," Eunice repeated.

He smiled to himself. He couldn't fool these two. They'd been best friends for decades and were as alike as two peas in a pod. Nosy. Bossy. With hearts as big as the outdoors. But that didn't mean he didn't find them trying sometimes.

"How can I not be nervous?" he asked, pushing his broad-brimmed straw hat off his forehead, hoping to catch a breeze. It was late May, not even summer yet, but as warm as an August day. "I haven't seen Lissie in ten years, but I've thought about her every single day."

"*Ya*, but mayhap she's thought of you all this time, too," Eunice offered thoughtfully.

"I doubt that." He frowned, raising an eyebrow behind his polarized sunglasses that had been all the talk in Faith's Run a few weeks back when neighbor Elzy Shroder called him out, declaring them too fancy. "Unless she was thinking of all the ways she'd tell me off if she saw me again."

His grandmother laughed. "Better than her not thinking about you at all."

He heard a motor vehicle approaching from behind and watched an old pickup truck slowly pass. Menno nodded to the driver. The elderly Englisher touched the brim of his ballcap in greeting, keeping a safe distance between his vehicle and the horse-drawn wagon. He had to be a local and not a tourist. The Amish and Englishers in Kent County didn't live the same life, but they coexisted nicely, for the most part.

"I'm still thinking you should have warned her I was living here," Menno said, directing his comment to Lissie's aunt, Eunice. Lissie and her children would move in with Eunice on the farm where she'd grown up. He watched the pickup increase speed and disappear around a bend into the woods.

"Saw no need to tell her," she answered firmly. "Who knows how she might have reacted? She's only been widowed a year. Her head's just coming back to her. She told me so in her letters." Eunice uttered a sound of annoyance, tugged on the tie of her black church bonnet and whipped it off. "Phew," she exclaimed, setting it on her lap. "I wanted to look nice for my niece and great-niece and nephew, but this will have to do in this heat." Her hand went to her prayer *kapp*, pinned in place.

Females in their Old Order community, young or old, wore their hair in a chignon beneath their *kapps*, but not Eunice. She had thick, snowy-white braids pinned crisscross at the back of her head, mostly covered by her black organza *kapp*. Occasionally, someone in their community would question if the style was *Plain* enough. However, their church district bishop knew Eunice had never been one to follow the straight and narrow. And his grandmother wasn't much better. Both were women of faith and good heart, but they had never quite fit into the conventionalities of Amish traditions. Some saw their nonconformance as a character flaw, but Menno considered it one of their best traits.

He glanced at Eunice. "I think you always look nice."

She flashed a toothy grin. "Save the flirting for my niece. She ought to be ripe for it. Her *ehemann* has been gone a year. God rest him. *The fool*," she added under her breath.

His grandmother tutted from the far side of the padded bench seat. She'd never said much about the man Lissie had married, but she'd made it clear she hadn't liked him.

"Mark my words," Eunice continued. "In no time, callers will be lined up at the door, hoping to walk out with her. She's a catch, my Lissie."

"Indeed she is," his grandmother agreed, pointing a knobby finger at him. "So, you best move fast."

Menno groaned. He couldn't wait to see Lissie again but was so scared that his hands were sweating. What if she wouldn't speak to him? Worse, what if she shouted at him right there at the bus stop? Lissie's temper had run hot back in their teenage years, and she had good reason to be angry with him now. He prayed she'd give him a chance to defend his actions. Or explain the reasons he did what he did. Surely, she'd forgive him once he explained why he left their Amish community without her all those years ago.

And maybe Guernsey cows would fall from the sky like manna from heaven.

He sighed, then shook his head with a grin. He had to stay positive. His love for Lissie had never wavered. If anything, it had grown stronger when he grew into adulthood and understood what it truly meant to love. Once he told her that, they could move on. At least he hoped so.

The county road took a sharp turn, and as the wagon went around the bend, he spotted the pickup that had passed them minutes ago pulling off to the side of the road. The denim overall–clad man hobbled toward the back of his pickup, leaning heavily on a cane.

"What's with this one?" Eunice asked, lifting her chin in the farmer's direction. "He best take care or he'll get flattened."

"*Ya*," their companion agreed. "Englishers drive too fast on this road. Like they're running one of those car races where you go round and round and get nowhere. NANCAR, they call it."

"NASCAR, Sheba," Eunice corrected.

His grandmother waved her friend off. "Either way, both are foolish names."

Accustomed to hearing the two women bicker, Menno gave them no mind. He slowed his horse, easing his wagon to a stop beside the pickup. "You all right?" he asked.

The man squinted in the bright sunlight. "Stupid flat."

Menno nodded, seeing the deflated rear tire now. "Can you call someone for help?" he asked.

The man waved off his suggestion. "Been changing my tires since I bought my first pickup in '51. A 1939 Ford 81C, it was."

Menno pulled his watch from a tiny pocket at the waistband of his trousers and groaned. Lissie's bus was expected in forty minutes, but it was another twenty to the bus station downtown. He exhaled loudly, eased the wagon forward and pulled in front of the truck. "I'm going to give him a hand," he told the women, hoping he wouldn't regret his decision. He didn't want to be late picking up Lissie. He couldn't be if he wanted to start on the right foot with her. But he couldn't leave this old man with a busted-down truck alongside the road. The farmer barely looked strong enough to lift a tire iron. How would he jack up the truck or lift his spare onto the axle?

"We don't want to be late," Eunice warned, the look on her face making it obvious she didn't approve of him stopping. "Else my niece is likely to be annoyed."

Menno grimaced. Annoyance he could deal with him, but if he knew Lissie, she'd be a sight more than annoyed.

More like infuriated if they were late. "We'll be on our way in no time." He wrapped the leather reins around the handbrake.

His grandmother tutted. "How do you know how to change a tire?" she demanded, clearly bothered he'd stopped to help.

He jumped down, landing on crumbly asphalt. He grabbed a pair of leather work gloves from under the wagon seat. "I learned a lot of things among the Englishers. Not all of it bad."

She muttered something under her breath, but he ignored her. "This won't take long," he said.

Menno truly thought it wouldn't take long. And it wouldn't have been if the farmer's jack hadn't been rusty, if the flat tire had not been so hard to get off, and if the elderly man had not dropped two lug nuts into the tall grass alongside the road. By the time Menno was back on his wagon seat, they'd be half an hour late to the bus stop. Thirty minutes, he thought as he pulled onto the road. Would half an hour ruin his plan to make amends with Lissie?

Not if he could help it.

Lissie Shetler stared at the huge bank sign across the street, which flashed the time and temperature in flickering red digits. It was eighty-one degrees and thirty-five minutes past when her aunt should have been there. She paced in front of the wooden bench outside the mini mart that doubled as a bus stop.

Where was her aunt? Lissie knew she'd been clear about the time of her arrival, and Eunice had written back confirming it. The octogenarian had admitted that at her age, she didn't drive all the way into town anymore, but she'd said a kind neighbor would bring her to fetch them. Had Eunice fallen ill? Lissie fretted. Had she *died*? She was, after all, in her eighties. Her chest tightened with dread. If something had happened to her aunt, there would have been no one to let Lissie know because no one in her hometown knew she was coming.

She glanced at her son and daughter sitting obediently on a bench, sharing a small bag of potato chips and a can of soda. She'd used money she couldn't spare on the treats because she couldn't stand the disappointment on her *kinner*'s faces when no one was there waiting for them after their long, uncomfortable journey. And now she had less than a hundred dollars to her name.

She glanced at the bank's digital clock again, wondering what to do. There was no way to call her aunt or anyone in the conservative Amish community where she'd grown up. Like many Old Order communities, she guessed many had landline phones in sheds on their property. A few men probably even had cell phones for work purposes. But she had no one's phone number. She'd had no contact with anyone outside her immediate family since she left as a new bride a decade ago.

She sighed, pulled a handkerchief from the black handbag on her elbow and mopped her brow. She was hot and thirsty. They'd drank all the water she'd packed for the trip, and she didn't dare spend more money to buy any. Hands on her hips, she glanced toward the street that led out of town and toward her family's farm. Should they just start walking home?

Home. That's how she'd begun to think of the old family farm in the weeks since she decided to accept her aunt's invitation and leave her hostile in-laws' house. She wasn't foolish enough to think the place would be anything like it had been when she left. Her parents had gone to the grave. Her oldest brother and his family had moved to Tennessee years ago. Only Eunice, her father's older sister, now lived there. But it was the only place Lissie had thought to go when she realized she and her children couldn't stay with their grandparents any longer. And Faith's Run, Delaware, was where she yearned to be. That was the place she'd been the happiest. Her childhood had been a good one, and it was here where she'd fallen in love with Menno.

The moment the thought of him popped into her head, she pushed it away. She would not let memories of him intrude. Not today, not ever again if she could help it. Every morning for the last ten years, she'd promised herself she would never give him a moment's thought again. And every night, she vowed to do better the next day.

Lissie took a deep breath of the hot, humid air that smelled of gasoline and rotting food from the overflowing trash barrel nearby. *Ya*, they'd walk, she decided. They'd start walking, and before they reached the county road, her aunt and the neighbor would no doubt show up, and Eunice would be bubbling with some explanation or another. Or maybe a kindly Amish family going her way would offer them a ride.

She turned to look at her children again. They had finished their snack and were fussing with each other as a brother and sister did. Seven-year-old Jonah was trying to climb onto one of their suitcases, and Naomi, who had just turned nine, was attempting to stop him before he hurt himself.

The suitcases. She groaned, staring at them. She planned to walk the eight miles or so with two travel-worn children and the bags that held everything she owned.

Against her will, tears sprang to her eyes. How did she think—

The sound of hoofbeats and wagon wheels caught her attention and she turned in that direction. It was an Amish horse and wagon. She couldn't see the wagon from where she stood, but someone was in a hurry. It had to be her aunt!

Breathing a sigh of relief, Lissie hurried to her children. "Your sister is right, Jonah. You shouldn't be on that," she chided gently, taking his hand. "Naomi, put the can and bag in the trash." She pointed to the barrel. "I think that's our Eunice coming now." She smiled down at them, and they excitedly smiled back.

Naomi picked up the discarded packaging from the bench, and Jonah snatched the can from her. "I'll throw 'em out," he declared.

Her daughter held the can just out of his reach. "I'm older. I should—"

"You can both do it," Lissie told them in her best *mam* voice. She turned to see a fine chestnut gelding pulling a nicer Amish wagon than she had ever seen in Ohio, where they had lived. She broke into a grin when she spotted Eunice in a lavender tab dress and black prayer *kapp* on the passenger side of the bench seat. She had not seen her aunt in ten years, but the woman did not look a day older. Murmuring a word of thanks to *Gott*, she waved.

Then Lissie's eyes locked with the Amish man driving the rig.

Her smile fell away as every drop of joy dissipated.

The driver looked like any other Old Order Amish man her age: straw hat, poly-denim trousers, short-sleeve shirt and suspenders. But he wasn't any other man.

It was Menno Bontrager. *Her* Menno.

Nay, not hers. She had thought once he was hers, but she'd been wrong. And not a day went by that she didn't regret that mistake.

"Lissie!" Eunice called, waving wildly as they pulled into the parking lot. "We're here! Sorry we're late, but an Englisher had a flat tire. He was an old man. Older than me, I'll warrant you. Needed a cane to walk. And I didn't want to stop, but this one—" She hooked her thumb in Menno's direction. "This one, always the Good Samaritan, insisted—"

Her aunt kept talking, but Lissie could only catch every other word. She felt her children move to her side.

Lissie's gaze fell on a third person in the wagon. The woman seated between her aunt and Menno was his maternal grandmother, Sheba Fisher.

"Our *endie*!" Jonah hollered in Pennsylvania *Deitsch*, bouncing in his black sneakers.

Naomi caught her brother's hand before he stepped in front of the moving wagon.

"Whoa," Menno called, pulling back hard on the reins as he rose. He halted the wagon right in front of her and looked down. "Lissie."

It was the sound of his voice more than him speaking her name that struck Lissie with such force that she suddenly felt uneasy on her feet. She took a shaky step back, wishing the bus hadn't left yet. If it were still there, she'd board it with her children. It wouldn't matter where it was going as long as she wasn't in the same town as Menno. But there was no bus, and she had nowhere to go even if there had been. Anger built up suddenly and bubbled over, hot and loud. "You!" she accused, pointing her finger at him. "What are you doing here?"

"*Endie*!" Jonah squealed and pulled away from Lissie.

"Jonah!" Naomi spoke sharply, going after her brother as he ran to the wagon to meet the great-aunt he'd heard so much about.

Lissie stared at Menno. For an instant, his face was one of pain and bewilderment. Then he smiled—the most handsome smile she had ever known.

"It's so good to see you. I'm here to pick you up and bring you all home." As he spoke, he secured the wagon's brake and reins.

Lissie took another unsteady step back as he leaped down from the wagon.

"Eunice doesn't like driving such a distance from home, so she asked me to—"

"*Nay*," Lissie interrupted, so angry that tears filled her eyes. "You are not supposed to be *here*!" She glanced up at her aunt, intending to demand why she would betray her this way, but she was busy greeting Jonah, who had just clambered up into the wagon.

Lissie returned her gaze to Menno. "I don't want you here. I didn't ever want to see you again."

Menno glanced at her children. Jonah had slid onto the back bench seat of his wagon. Both women were fussing over him in a mixture of English and Pennsylvania *Deitsch*. Naomi scrambled into the wagon after her little brother.

He returned his gaze to Lissie. "Can we not do this here?" he asked quietly.

"Not do this here?" she demanded. Her anger was threatening to become rage. Suddenly, all the disappointment, the sadness and the loneliness of the past decade were forcing their way out. "You don't want to do it here?" she demanded. "Where shall we do it then, Menno? Shall we do it there?" She pointed to the space beside her. "Or there?" She pointed to the trash can. "Or maybe we should do it in there?" She pointed to the store's glass door.

He tried to catch her hand, and she pulled it away, certain his touch would burn her. "Where would you like to do this, Menno?"

"I know we need to talk, but—"

Refusing to listen to him, she spoke over him, continuing her rant. "I have an idea. How about—"

"Lissie!" he shouted over her.

The store's door flew open, and the clerk who had patiently waited while she paid for the children's snack in dimes and nickels stepped out, holding a cellphone in his hand.

Lissie and Menno both went quiet.

"Everything all right here?" The clerk eyed them. "Or do I need to call the cops?"

"Sorry. No, no need to call the police." Menno held up his hand. "Sorry," he repeated. "We just…" He lamely pointed to Lissie. "Family stuff."

Lissie's eyes widened. *Family stuff?* How dare he call himself family! She was about to correct Menno when he grabbed her hand, his look one of warning. He held her gaze a second longer and then turned to the clerk. "I apologize. We're going. I'll grab the suitcases and we'll be on our way."

The clerk looked at Lissie. "You all right, ma'am?"

She hesitated. She was so furious that her first impulse was to shout at him, too. To ask him if things looked all right—two Amish folks hollering in a public parking lot. But she bit her tongue, ashamed she had caused such a stir. This was a private matter between her and Menno. It wasn't meant to be heard by Englishers, Sheba, Eunice or the children. She felt her cheeks grow hot with embarrassment. Worse, she was beginning to tear up. "I'm right enough."

The clerk hesitated. "You sure?"

She nodded, not trusting herself to speak.

"All righty, but if you're not waiting for the bus and not buying anything…" He pointed to a large sign warning against loitering.

"We're on our way." Menno walked past her to pick up one of their suitcases in each hand. "Going now!"

Shaking his head, the clerk walked back inside.

Lissie grabbed the other suitcase, the largest of the three, and wheeled it to the back of the wagon.

"Everything *oll recht, mam*?" Naomi asked, her voice uncertain as she peered down from the wagon. Her gaze flicked to Menno and then back at her mother.

"Everything's fine," Lissie responded, gentling her tone. "We'll soon be on our way."

Naomi dropped onto the rear bench, and Lissie grabbed her battered suitcase with two hands and lifted it into the air. Menno tried to take it from her, but she shot him a warning look over the top, and he took a step back, raising both hands in surrender. She barely managed to get the heavy suitcase up and over the backboard of the wagon, and when she released it, it fell hard on top of the others.

Out of breath, she dropped her hands to her hips. She met Menno's gaze and had to swallow back tears. She had been so angry at him for a long time for abandoning her, but she thought she'd moved past it. Gotten over *him*. But this tightening in her chest reminded her of what she had probably always known. She hadn't.

"Let's go home," Menno said softly. He had removed his fancy Englisher sunglasses, and she saw his bright blue eyes. He offered his hand. "Let me help you up."

She stared at his hand. She was so worn out physically and emotionally from the years with a man she should never have married, from his death and the days that had followed with his awful parents. She was so tired that she desperately wanted to take Menno's hand. She wanted to share her life's burdens with someone. But not Menno. It couldn't be him. Not ever again.

"Lissie." He moved his hand impatiently. "Let's get your *kinner* home. They must be exhausted." He met her eyes again. "I can see you are, too."

She shook her head, taking a step away from him. "*Nay*, I'll not ride with you," she spat softly. It was the only way she could deal with him right now—with anger. Otherwise, she'd break into a thousand pieces.

"Really?" He pushed his sunglasses back on. "You won't ride with me? Then exactly how do you intend to get home?"

"I'll walk."

"*Eight miles*?" he asked, frustration in his tone.

Twelve hundred miles if I have to, she thought.

And then she started for home.

Chapter Two

Menno watched in disbelief as Lissie strode away. His emotions were all a jumble. He was so happy to see her that he felt lightheaded, yet her reaction to his presence also exasperated him. He knew she'd be angry with him, but he'd hoped she would have mellowed a bit. Didn't marriage and motherhood do that to a woman?

Not this woman.

He crossed his arms over his chest, observing her determined stride and how her handbag swung on her elbow. There was no arguing that she was a sight to behold, even in her fury. She appeared ordinary in her tab dress, black canvas sneakers and a white organza prayer *kapp*, like other women wore in their Old Order community. But there was nothing else ordinary about his Lissie. She was taller than most women he knew, not heavy but possessing a sturdiness he had always appreciated. She was no waif who couldn't haul a five-gallon bucket of water or climb down from a buggy without assistance. And her hair—it was her hair he dreamed of, how smooth and sweet-smelling it had been between his fingers. Seeing stray tendrils of nutmeg brown at the nape of her neck glistening gold in the sunlight made his heart skip a beat.

His mouth suddenly dry, Menno snapped himself out

of his musing. While he contemplated her beauty, she was getting away. "Lissie, will you please be sensible?" he called, watching her move across the parking lot, arms pumping, putting more distance between them with every moment. "Lissie!" he repeated louder.

"I'm being *perfectly* sensible," she shouted, turning her head enough for him to see her profile. She had a long, slender nose and high cheekbones, which had turned bright red. "I'm going home!"

She had aged in the last ten years, in a good way. The pretty, soft roundness of acne-dimpled youth had been replaced by more defined features and lightly freckled skin. Her eyes were big and brown, flecked with gold and fringed by thick lashes. She was gorgeous, his Lissie.

Menno glanced over his shoulder at the wagon. Sheba, Eunice, and Lissie's children watched Lissie's escape with great interest, as did the shopkeeper. He was outside again, his tattooed arms crossed and a silly grin on his face as he enjoyed the spectacle. Most Amish women didn't act this way in public, especially in front of Englishers. But Lissie wasn't like most Amish women.

His gaze shifted to her little ones. They didn't seem frightened to be left with strangers, or surprised by their mother's outburst or her walking away. If he had to guess, they'd seen her like this before. Some things never changed, did they?

He looked back at Lissie, unsure of what to do. Did he go after her? Was that what she wanted?

She was nearly to the street. "Lissie," he called again in exasperation. "Your children." He indicated the *kinner* with his hand.

"Naomi and Jonah, mind your *endie*," Lissie instructed, ignoring him. "I'll see you at the house." Then she disappeared around the cement block building.

Now what? Menno swept off his straw hat and wiped his brow with a handkerchief.

"What do you think you're doing?" his grandmother called. *"Kinnskind!"* Grandchild.

He turned.

Sheba rose, arms spread wide. Like many older Amish, she wore photosensitive wire-frame glasses that darkened in the bright sun. Hers were identical to Eunice's. "I said, what do you think you're doing?" she demanded impatiently.

"I..." Menno stuffed his hat back on his head. "I don't know," he admitted as he walked toward the wagon. "What am I *supposed* to do?"

She gestured dramatically to the empty driver's seat beside her. When he'd had his back to them, Eunice had somehow managed to climb into the rear of the wagon. She was now seated between her great-niece and great-nephew, chattering away in Pennsylvania *Deitsch* as if nothing unusual was happening.

"What do you do? You go after her," his grandmother said, speaking to him as if he were a child again.

He started to head in Lissie's direction.

"Not on foot!" she exclaimed. Then she mumbled something about men that wasn't too complimentary.

Menno hurried back to the wagon and swung up. His driving horse, Clyde, seemed as eager to catch up with Lissie as he was and took off when Menno gave him the go-ahead. They wheeled out of the parking lot and onto the street, going so fast that Jonah gave a whoop of excitement as the wagon nearly stood on two wheels. His grandmother grabbed the side of the seat to keep her balance, but grinned.

Around the corner, Menno spotted Lissie half a block ahead on the sidewalk. A pickup truck was between them, so it took another two blocks before the truck turned off, allowing him to catch up with her. "*Oll recht*, Lissie, you made your point." He drove the wagon beside her, keeping an eye on the traffic. "I get it. You're angry with me." She was walking so fast that more hair had escaped her *kapp*, creating a nutmeg-and-gold halo around her head. It was distracting.

"I know you have a right to be upset with me," he continued, rising to his feet. "Now, would you please get in the wagon?"

"Careful with your tone," his grandmother counseled. "You're the one who wronged her in the first place."

He scowled. "Sheba, I know I—" He cut himself off and returned his attention to the love of his life trying to get away from him. "Please, Lissie? Please get in the wagon."

"*Nay*," she shouted.

His grandmother chuckled. "You knew this wasn't going to be easy, Menno. Strongheaded, that one."

"Always was," Eunice chimed in from the back seat. "Reminds me of myself when I was her age."

Menno groaned. He adored his grandmother, whom he'd been calling by her first name at her insistence, since she moved in with them when he was a kid. He felt the same way about Eunice. But sometimes, he wished they would sit quietly in rocking chairs and knit like other *grossmammis*.

He looked ahead, tightening his hands on the well-worn leather reins. The sidewalk would end at the next intersection. They'd soon be out of town.

"Really, Lissie? You're going to walk all the way home?" Menno said.

"*Ya*, I am. Please take my aunt and children home." She stepped off the curb, and a car to their left waited for her to cross.

Once the vehicle passed, he rolled through the intersection onto the narrower road with a few Englisher houses. Lissie ignored him and kept walking.

"Now what?" he muttered, sitting hard on the bench seat.

Eunice patted him on the shoulder from behind. "Give her a minute," she encouraged quietly. "You know how she is when she gets riled."

He nodded, forcing himself to calm down. He drove the wagon for five minutes beside Lissie, holding the horse back to match her pace. Cars and trucks passed them, their occupants staring with curiosity. He didn't speak to her, and she didn't speak to him. She wouldn't even look at him.

Another five minutes went by. Everyone in the wagon acted as if there was nothing odd about riding along beside a grown woman who chose to walk instead of ride. Finally, he could stand it no longer. "You sure this is what you want, Lissie?" he asked, keeping all his emotions out of his tone. "You want to *walk* to Faith's Run?"

"It's not that I *want* to walk. I'd love to ride." She turned her head to meet his gaze, her brown eyes fiery with anger. "I just don't want to ride with *you*."

"Li—" He closed his mouth. Her aunt was right. If there was one thing he knew about Lissie, it was that sometimes there was no arguing with her. It had been that way when they were kids and later in their teenage years when they fell in love. When she got like this, she was irrational. Nothing was to be done until she cooled off, and only then could they have a reasonable discussion.

"Fine," he mumbled. "Have it your way." He gave the young gelding free rein and drove past her.

They were six wagon lengths ahead of Lissie when seven-year-old Jonah said, "Are we leaving *mam*?" He sounded more curious than worried.

Menno glanced over his shoulder to see Naomi, a miniature of her mother, patting her brother's knee. "*Ya*, but we'll see her at the house, won't we, *Endie*?" The little girl smiled up at Eunice.

"That we will," Eunice agreed happily.

And maybe Eunice was right. Maybe Lissie was actually going to walk the next seven miles.

But Lissie quickly fell behind, even though Menno kept his horse to a walk, which would make the trip twice as long as it had to be. The farther they got from town, the more distance grew between the wagon and Lissie. As they rode, the passengers engaged in a steady conversation, with the women asking curious questions of the children and the little ones answering as best they could. Menno waited for Lissie to call out to him, asking him to wait so she could join them in the wagon. But it didn't happen.

Four miles and an hour from town, he lost sight of Lissie and eased off the road into an abandoned driveway overgrown and thick with pin oak and maple trees. It was a good fifteen minutes before Lissie caught up to them.

Menno met her gaze as she stopped beside the wagon's rear wheel. The hair falling from her organza prayer *kapp* was damp with perspiration and stuck to her face, and she looked exhausted.

He could see that her resolve was flagging.

Her dark brown eyes held his for a long moment—so long that he wondered if she was waiting for *him* to say something. But what did she want him to say? That he was sorry? Of course, he was sorry that he had left her without saying goodbye. He was sorry it had taken him so long to get his life together and know what he wanted. But this wasn't the time or the place for that discussion.

Finally, she broke eye contact. Without saying a word, she handed her handbag to her aunt and used the wagon wheel as a step. She climbed into the back, settled on the seat and pulled her boy onto her lap. Menno kept his mouth shut as he eased the wagon onto the road, but it felt like a win.

Or at least a start.

As the wagon rolled onto the pavement and they headed for home, Lissie sighed with relief and leaned back on the bench seat, wrapping her arms around her son. She was hot and tired and angry. She was as angry as she'd ever been in her life, and she'd been plenty angry the last ten years. She'd been angry with Menno, with her late husband and with her in-laws. But mostly, she was angry with herself for all the bad decisions she'd made and continued to make.

And here she was with another mistake weighing heavy on her shoulders. She shouldn't have come back to Faith's Run. But never in her wildest dreams had she considered the possibility that Menno might have returned to the community. She assumed he was somewhere far from Delaware driving a big red pickup and living the life of an Englisher. Why hadn't she asked about Menno before bringing her children here?

She couldn't believe her aunt had been so devious. Eunice had mentioned a kind neighbor in her letters several times over the past year, but hadn't revealed who it was. And Lissie had been so caught up in her misery that she hadn't thought to ask. Now here she was, being forced to accept a ride home with the last person she ever wanted to see again.

Naomi slipped her small, damp hand into Lissie's and looked anxiously into her mother's face. Guilt washed over Lissie. She would have to apologize to her daughter later for her behavior at the bus stop. But for now, all Lissie could do was squeeze her little girl's hand and offer a smile. "We'll be at the house in half an hour," she whispered in her daughter's ear.

Jonah wiggled off Lissie's lap and grabbed the backrest of the front bench seat. She realized what he was doing a second too late, and before she could grab the waistband of his trousers, he was up and over, dropping down between Menno and his grandmother. "*Nay*, Jonah, stay—" She dropped her hands to her lap, knowing it would be petty to insist he return to her lap rather than let him sit beside Menno. Her children knew nothing of her and Menno's past.

"There we go," Sheba declared, grabbing Jonah's straw hat as it tumbled off his head. The hat was identical to Menno's, right down to the leather band above the brim, just smaller.

Menno looked down at Jonah and smiled. Her son beamed and scooted a bit closer to him. At seven, Jonah was reaching the age where he wanted to be with other boys and men, rather than being coddled by females.

"You think I could hold the reins?" Jonah asked.

Lissie tugged on a lock of her son's dark hair that fell shaggy to his shoulders. "It's not polite to ask such a thing. Of a stranger," she added, glaring at the back of Menno's head.

"*Nay*, it's fine," Menno said, not looking at her. Instead, his attention was on her son. "I hope we won't be strangers now that you're moving to Faith's Run. He ought to start learning how to drive a rig. I was driving one by the time I was his age."

"You were?" Jonah asked, his eyes filled with awe and admiration.

Menno surveyed the newly sprouted soybean fields on both sides of them, then glanced over his shoulder to check for traffic. "We're on a straightaway with no vehicles coming or going. Here you go." He moved to give her son the reins. "Let me show you how to hold them."

Jonah's eyes grew as round as supper plates. "Really? I can drive?"

Menno shrugged. "You can give it a try. Just keep us out of the ditch."

"My *dat* never let me hold the reins," Jonah breathed, still gazing up at Menno.

The tone of her son's voice made Lissie flinch. Then Menno gently laid the leathers in her son's hand and her heart swelled. Jonah spoke the truth. Her late husband, Alvan, had never allowed their son to even pretend to drive a wagon or a buggy. The man had never smiled at their son the way Menno was smiling at him right now—with approval. Kindness.

Lissie's eyes suddenly filled with tears and she had to look away. "Just for a minute, Jonah," she said, hoping no one heard the emotion in her voice. "Then give the reins back to Menno."

She nearly choked when she spoke his name and fumbled for a handkerchief in her pocketbook. It wasn't in her nature to be so emotional. She didn't usually waste time feeling things. She was a doer. And what she was going to do now, she didn't know. She couldn't stay in Faith's Run with Menno living there. But where would she go? Returning to Ohio wasn't an option. She'd known that when she considered it back at the bus stop.

As she considered her next move, the miles and minutes to the home where she'd grown up passed quickly. Her aunt and Sheba kept up a steady chatter with the children and Menno made no attempt to speak to her. Before she knew it, they were pulling into the gravel lane that led to her family's farmhouse fifty yards off the road.

A slight breeze blew across her face, lifting her spirits as she took in her surroundings. She was shocked by how little had changed in a decade. The two-story L-shaped white clapboard farmhouse with three redbrick chimneys looked the same. So did the large barn and various outbuildings. Even the wood-and-metal windmill, with its blades slowly turning high above the well-house, was unchanged. It was as if life here in Faith's Run had stood still while she was gone.

Nay, the place looked better. The missing shutter on the second floor at the west end of the house that had been gone since her childhood had been replaced. The lawn was brilliant with green grass that had been recently mowed, and flower beds and shrubbery lined the house's foundation. As they passed the front and came to the large rear addition, she saw that the back porch had been rebuilt and expanded with a portion screened in.

She was shocked when she spotted the *dawdi* house in the distance, which had been little more than a shack and used for storage when she left. The small grandfather's house had been completely remodeled. It had new siding and a new front porch with rocking chairs. There were flower beds there, too, filled with multicolored pansies. She squinted to get a better look at something red hanging above the porch's railing. The Amish didn't use red in clothing or their home; it was too fancy. Was that a *hummingbird feeder*?

She sat back on the wagon seat, dumbfounded. After her husband died and Lissie had begun writing to her aunt, she had assumed Eunice lived in the *dawdi* house. Her eldest brother had rented out the family farm when he and his family, along with their parents, had moved to Tennessee eight years ago. Both their *mam* and *dat* had passed away within a year of the move. Lissie had heard through a distant cousin that part of the rental agreement was that Eunice had been able to remain on the farm. Lissie had assumed her aunt lived in the *dawdi* house. But then, in a letter, Eunice had said she was now in the big house again. Lissie had asked how that had come to be, but she hadn't responded, and Lissie figured that she'd hear all the details when she arrived.

Had her aunt somehow managed to buy the family farm? That made no sense. Where would she have gotten the money to buy the place? Where had the money come from to fix up the property? Eunice had been made a childless widow at twenty-one and never remarried. And how was her aunt taking care of all this? Eunice had mentioned that a local boy—meaning Amish—helped her care for what little livestock she still had, but surely he wasn't mowing the lawn and weeding flower beds. A fourteen-year-old boy had plenty of his own chores on his family's farm, especially this time of year with planting.

"Eunice," Lissie breathed, trying to temper her shock so as not to insult her elder. "How have you been able to—"

"And here we are," Menno announced cheerfully, guiding the horse to a hitching rail.

They parked in front of a huge lilac bush that had been little more than a twig when she had moved to Ohio. The pale purple blooms drifted on the warm spring air with their fragrance, and her mind was suddenly filled with happy memories. She had loved this farm and her life here. Only after Menno left did it become too painful to stay here.

"Yay!" Jonah shouted, throwing his arms into the air. "We're home! Our new home."

"Our new home," Naomi repeated, her voice soft but excited.

Menno jumped down, taking Jonah with him. Together, they moved in front of the gelding to tie him to the hitching post.

"Will you come in for iced tea?" Eunice asked Sheba as she rose.

Realizing her aunt was about to get down from the wagon on her own, Lissie quickly climbed down and rounded the rear to offer her hand.

Sheba leaned on the back of the seat to talk to her friend. "I'd like to. I'm sure this one has lots to say." She gestured to Lissie. "But I imagine my grandson will be eager to get me home and check on things at the shop. He hired a new girl, and I hear she can't tell butter pecan from rocky road. Pretty enough, but daft." She tapped her temple.

Lissie looked from one elderly woman to the other. It sounded like they were talking about ice cream, but she wasn't following. What did Menno have to do with ice cream?

Studying her aunt, Lissie pointed to her handbag in the back of the wagon and Naomi grabbed it before climbing down. In a hurry to get her suitcases out of the back before Menno tried to help, she heaved one after the other to the ground. Thankfully, Jonah was chattering about a grasshopper he'd found on a bush at one of the rest stops and had Menno's full attention.

"Take the rolly one," Lissie instructed her daughter. "Pull it to the porch steps. I'll carry it up." As she spoke, she grabbed one large suitcase in each hand and lifted them both at once. They were so heavy she couldn't lift them more than an inch above the ground, but somehow, she was able to move forward with them.

"It was good to see you, Sheba," Lissie called, forcing a smile. Under different circumstances, it truly *would* have been nice to see her; she had always liked the quirky woman. Even in her anger, Lissie knew that a grandmother wasn't responsible for her grandson's sins. But she was hot and tired and wanted to escape Menno as quickly as possible. She intended to settle her little ones in the house, feed them supper, let them bathe and tuck them into bed. Maybe then she could catch her breath and decide what to do now that she knew Menno lived with her. She didn't have the strength to return to her in-laws', but surely there was somewhere else she and the children could go. Perhaps she could even persuade Eunice to join them.

"Jonah!" Lissie called. "Come along and help me get these suitcases into the house."

Her boy and Menno turned to her.

"Let me get those for you," Menno said, starting for the porch.

"Menno," Sheba said from the wagon. "Let's go."

He looked up at his grandmother, pointing toward Lissie. "I was just going to—"

"*Let's go,*" Sheba said sharply. "I'm tired and I want my supper."

Sheba then said something more quietly to him, something Lissie didn't catch because she turned away from him to drag the bags up the steps.

"*Sohn,*" Lissie called without looking over her shoulder.

Lissie heard the rumble of Menno's voice. He was saying something to Jonah. Then the boy came running.

"Bye!" Jonah said excitedly. "Bye! See you soon."

As Lissie staggered up the steps, Jonah joined his sister.

Lissie heard Menno get into the wagon.

"Good to see you, Lissie," he called.

Ignoring him, Lissie took the last step to the porch and dropped both bags with a huff of exhaustion. Her eyes burned, and she suddenly felt like she would burst into tears. She had been so careful planning this move—to create a fresh start with her little ones in a place where they would be loved. How could this have gone so wrong already?

"I'll see you soon, Lissie," Menno called, sounding as hopeful as Jonah.

Lissie swallowed back her tears. "Not if I can help it," she muttered under her breath. Then she entered the house, letting the screen door slam behind her.

Chapter Three

His grandmother didn't say a word, and Menno was grateful. He wasn't surprised by Lissie's initial reaction to seeing him again, but he was disappointed. He knew he'd hurt her terribly when he'd left their Amish community of Faith's Run, but leaving her behind had been the right decision. He truly believed that. Still, he'd misjudged how angry she would be—and underestimated how deeply he still loved her.

He drove his wagon from the gravel lane onto the paved country road and headed west. It was two miles to his mother's house, where his grandmother lived, which he hoped would give him enough time to process what had happened today. He glanced at his grandmother, who was watching him. He sensed she was waiting for him to speak.

"I knew she'd still be angry with me, but I didn't think she'd be this furious," he said quietly. "Not after so many years."

"I did." Sheba swept her black bonnet from under the seat and pulled it over her prayer *kapp*, leaving the grosgrain ties to flutter in the breeze.

He sighed and listened to the rhythmic clip-clop of the standardbred's hooves. He had never been a man given to glumness, not even in the darker moments when he lived among the English. But right now, he was fighting a feeling of hopelessness. Would all his planning, hard work, and dream of fulfilling his promise to Lissie when he was eighteen be for naught? Had he been foolish to believe he could ever make it up to her for what he had done?

That fear weighed heavy on his heart, and he let several minutes pass without speaking before asking, "Why does everything in life have to be so hard?"

Sheba chuckled, a blend of humor and wisdom in her laugh. "Because straight is the gate, and narrow is the way."

He'd never been one to quote the Bible. Half the time, he had no idea of the meaning of the passages the preachers read on Sunday mornings. But he knew right from wrong. He loved God, and he'd led a righteous life. He was a man of faith above all else. "I have no idea what those words mean," he admitted.

"It means life is hard," Sheba responded, now exasperated.

She looked away and for a time, they both watched a pair of cardinals, the male bright red and the female a more subtle shade of rust and brown, alight on the branch of a loblolly pine tree near the road. Cardinals chose their mates for life, just like people, he mused. And even after the day's events, he still hoped to convince Lissie that they were meant to be together. Even if the path there was narrow.

Menno ran his fingers over the smooth leather of the reins and glanced at his grandmother again. Sheba was a tiny woman, thin and frail in appearance, but nothing was frail about her mind or body. She could put in a day of housework and cooking and beat him at three games of checkers in a row. She never ran out of energy. Or advice.

"What do I do now?" he asked.

"Do? You take me home."

Did she think this was the time to be funny? he wondered in frustration. "I *mean*, what do I do about Lissie?"

"You keep to your plan. You show her how you've changed. But also how you haven't," she warned, raising an arthritic finger beneath his nose. "You show her that you can provide for her and her children. That you *want* to. You show her—not just tell her—that you still love her. Let us not love in word or talk but in deed and truth."

It was another Bible verse, but at least it was easy to understand. Despite his disappointing day, Menno found himself smiling. "You're right. Stick with the plan. Good advice. *Danki*." He looked at her over the rim of his sunglasses. "Not many men can say that their grandmother is one of their best friends."

"Not many men have someone like me for a grandmother." Looking past him, she pointed. "Pull in there."

Across the road, three buggies and nine cars had managed to squeeze into the gravel parking lot of his ice cream shop, which was meant for half as many. Amish and English customers were getting in and out of their vehicles, laughing, talking and enjoying the sunny afternoon. From one of the cars, he heard a country song playing. A calmness fell over Menno as he was reminded of how blessed he was.

Bontrager's Ice Creamery was more successful than he could have ever imagined. Amish and English folks had come from miles to visit the little white cement block building with giant ice cream cones painted on the exterior walls. When he moved back to Faith's Run three years ago, he'd worked for his brother Jude in the dairy business alongside their two younger brothers, but soon came up with the idea of making ice cream and selling it from a roadside stand. No one in the community had believed the dream was viable. Even his family had doubts, but they all supported him. Now he was earning enough money to buy property, support his family and tithe generously to the church.

"Why do you want to stop here?" Menno asked. "Back at Eunice's, you acted like you couldn't wait to get home." Menno pulled off onto the shoulder rather than crossing the road into the parking lot. Several motor vehicles passed them. "I thought you said you needed to get home to rest."

"Why would I need to rest?" she scoffed. "I've done nothing but ride around all day in this wagon. I only said that to get you into the buggy before you made things worse by chasing that girl into the house. You couldn't see that the waterworks were about to start."

He drew back, silently chastising himself for not noticing that Lissie had been about to cry. He didn't want to make her cry ever again.

"*Whelp*, neither here nor there now," Sheba continued. "But I need to get home to put supper on the table. Your *mam* had a full day of appointments. We'll be blessed to see her at the table tonight."

His mother, Elizabeth, had the unusual occupation of midwife and maintained an office in their home. After training as a nurse midwife in Canada, she married his father and settled in Delaware. While higher education was uncommon among the Amish in Kent County, their bishop had granted her a dispensation because of the urgent need for midwifery in home births. She had been permitted to continue her career and was still practicing thirty years later.

"If you want to get home, why are we stopping here?" Menno asked his grandmother, thoroughly confused.

"Because I know you want to see how the new girl you hired is doing. So get out." She raised her chin in dismissal.

"But there's no place to park," he told her, indicating the packed lot. "And you can't wait for me here on the road. It's not safe." As if to confirm his statement, a pickup truck flew by far faster than the posted speed limit. He eyed his ice cream shop's service window, where folks waited in line. "I need to check on things, but I can take you home and walk back."

She slid toward him on the bench, pushing him with her bony hip. "Do what you must, then come to the house for supper."

"Are you sure you don't want me to drive you up?" He lifted his chin toward the house that looked similar to Lissie's family home but larger and set farther back on the road.

"You think I can't still drive a horse and wagon?" his grandmother railed, grabbing the leathers from his hand. "My eyesight's going on me, but it's not that bad yet. Go on with you. The sooner you're done here, the sooner we can eat. That taco casserole I made up this morning is going into the oven directly."

Half thinking she might push him out if he didn't get a move on, Menno jumped down.

"See you up at the house!" she called as she clicked to his gelding, and the wagon rolled forward.

"Careful of the traffic when you cross!" he warned. Then he jogged across the street, eager to finish his business here, have supper with his family and get home.

* * *

When Lissie closed the door leading into the mudroom of her childhood home, she shut it on Menno and all the emotions tied to their past. She shifted into *mam* mode. While Eunice pulled out containers from the refrigerator for dinner, Lissie, Naomi and Jonah carried their bags upstairs. Due to her bad knees, Eunice slept downstairs in what had once been the parlor, leaving four upstairs bedrooms of various sizes for Lissie to use as she wished. Although her first impulse was to take the room she had shared years ago with her much older sister, Gertie, she gave it to Naomi and her brother's room to Jonah. There were too many memories of lying in her bed, dreaming of a life with Menno. Instead, she wheeled her suitcase into her parents' old room.

After a supper of chicken salad on biscuits and time spent talking about the bus ride from Ohio and what kind of food Naomi and Jonah liked, Lissie sent her children off to bed. While her original idea was for them to sleep in their own rooms, Jonah became teary-eyed when he found out he wouldn't be with his sister. In all fairness, he had never slept in a room alone since the day he was born. When Naomi admitted she wanted her brother with her, Lissie let him climb into the second twin bed in her daughter's room. Eventually, she would need to separate them, but she knew this was a matter to be settled another day. Once her children were tucked in, Lissie sat on Jonah's bed and sang an old hymn in High German, and they both fell asleep within minutes.

Carrying a battery lantern that Eunice had thoughtfully placed on the nightstand in each bedroom, Lissie descended the staircase, listening to the creak of each pine step she knew by heart. Her life had changed substantially since she had been here last. Yet some things never changed, which gave her comfort.

"That was quick," Eunice called as Lissie reached the bottom of the staircase.

"They were exhausted." Lissie turned off the lantern and left it on a small table in the main hall. The hall led to the kitchen, the front door, the living room, a bathroom and Eunice's bedroom, which had once been the sewing room.

When Lissie entered the kitchen, she found her aunt at the large porcelain sink up to her elbows in dishwater.

"I said I'd take care of the dishes as soon as I got downstairs, *Endie*," Lissie chastised gently. She dropped an apron from a wooden peg on the wall over her dress. "What kind of guest would I be if I let you do all the cleanup?"

"You're not a guest. This is your home. And there wasn't much to *rett* up," Eunice said. "What's wrong with those two? I've never seen children eat so neatly. Nary a crumb on the floor for me to broom."

Lissie knew her aunt didn't mean to sound critical, given the concern in her voice. Lissie had heard similar comments before. People remarked that her children were too quiet, too clean, too cautious, and not like other *kinner*. Naomi and Jonah *were* all those things; they'd had to be. It was what her in-laws expected, and they'd had to follow the rules of the home when they were forced to move in with them two years ago.

"Sit," Lissie said. "I'll make you some chamomile tea. You look tired."

"Not as tired as you," Eunice said, but she stepped from the sink and stripped off her bright pink dishwashing gloves. "I'll have tea, but only if you join me." She smiled slyly. "And we could have an oatmeal cookie or two. They have dried cherries instead of raisins. You'll love them. And we can talk," she added. "About…*things*."

Lissie walked over to the propane stove to turn on the burner underneath the teakettle, giving herself a moment. She knew what Eunice wanted to talk about—Menno. But she wasn't sure if she could discuss him calmly. It had been a shock to see him again. She'd meant it when she said she wouldn't have come home if she'd known he was here. She didn't know what she would do now. She'd decided to return to Faith's Run when her in-laws began pressuring her to marry her deceased husband's twenty-year-old brother. It felt wrong on so many levels that she'd impulsively chosen to return to Delaware, and she hadn't wavered in her decision—until now. And it was all Menno's fault.

Not ready to have a conversation about him, Lissie said, "*Ya*, we do need to talk. About the arrangements here. As I said in my letters, I don't expect you to care for us financially." *While we're here*, she thought. *Until I figure out where to go now.* "I'm going to take over the housework and get a job."

"Get a job!" Eunice exclaimed, as if that was the most ridiculous idea she'd ever heard.

But with less than a hundred dollars in her wallet, Lissie needed money to buy food and necessities for herself and the children. Back in Ohio, her father-in-law had refused to allow her to work outside his home. That meant she'd had to ask him for anything she or the children needed, right down to personal necessities, and even then, the purchases were made *for* her. She wasn't permitted to go to a store. It had been fourteen months since she'd bought a tube of toothpaste or a pair of socks, which was not only humiliating, but demeaning. In the months after the shock of Alvan's death and her in-laws completely taking over her and her children's lives, Lissie had felt like she was losing what little bit of identity she had left. It wasn't until she decided to move in with Eunice that she felt the slimmest thread of who she was return to her.

"You don't need a job," Eunice protested as Lissie rinsed off the last plate and set it on the drainboard. "The cellar is full of canned fruit and veggies and I've got a freezer of meat."

Lissie didn't know if she was more surprised by her aunt's propane freezer or that, at her age, she was still growing and canning vegetables. "You still grow a full garden?" she asked, drying her hands on a muslin dish towel on her way to the dish cupboard.

Eunice laughed as she plopped down into one of the sturdy, mismatched chairs at the kitchen table. Some had been replaced over the decade, but Lissie recognized several. And the big pine trestle table was the one her *dat* had made.

"Do I look like a woman who likes to hoe?" her aunt asked humorously. "*Ya*, I scratch a little in the garden because I still like to get my hands dirty, but I buy my veggies from the neighbors. Or at Walmart," she added. "And people are always bringing me food. Neighbors, friends. Someone is always dropping off a bag of potatoes or a jar of peaches. Same for meat. Whenever someone sends a pig or a cow to the Haases' butcher shop, I get a package of this or that. Elizabeth is the worst one. She's always giving me food."

Elizabeth was Menno's mother, a woman Lissie had adored her whole life. When Lissie was young, she'd wished Elizabeth had been her mother instead of his. Elizabeth Bontrager had been all a little girl, and later, a young woman, could have wanted in a mother. She was warm and kind and always eager to hear what Lissie had to say. She offered her opinion, too, but usually only when asked. Lissie's mother was never unkind, and Lissie knew she had loved her children in her way, but the woman who'd had Lissie late in life had always been distant, as if offspring were an annoyance to be tolerated.

Lissie carried two mugs and a tin of teabags to the table. "You don't know how much my two can eat," she said, trying to make a joke out of the situation. She didn't want to voice how demoralizing it was for her to be unable to provide for her children. "I want to pay our way." She poured water from the kettle into the mugs on the table. "*Endie*, I *need* to pay my own way." Against her will, her voice cracked.

"I'm sorry you lost your husband and the children lost a father." Eunice rose and returned to the table, carrying a tin box. "But I'd be a liar if I told you I liked that Alvan. I knew he wasn't right for you when I met him." She sat down and cracked open the cookie tin. The sweet, rich smell of oats, brown sugar and cinnamon filled the air. "I told you not to marry him."

She *had* told her not to marry Alvan. Lissie remembered the conversation well. A lump rose in her throat as she dropped the herbal teabags from their container into the mugs.

"But I know why you did it," Eunice continued. She took a big bite of the cookie then shook it at her. "Young and impulsive, you were. Just like Menno, taking off like that. Worrying his mother half to death. It's a good thing it took him years to make his way back here. Otherwise, I might have given him a good slap." She took another bite. "'Course I'd have had to get in line behind Sheba and Elizabeth to do it."

Under other circumstances, Lissie might have laughed. Her aunt had always had a way with words, but she wasn't in a laughing mood. Menno living in Faith's Run was a huge problem because she wasn't sure the town was big enough for them both.

"You should have told me he was here, Eunice." Lissie hesitated. "I don't know that we can stay."

"I don't want to hear such nonsense. You're not going anywhere. This is your home now," Eunice said. "And why didn't I tell you he was living here? Because I knew you wouldn't have come. That's why." She sounded impatient with Lissie now. "You're still young and impulsive. You showed me that today." She leaned back in her chair, shaking her head. "I was half hoping you might walk all the way here from town. Might have given you time to find the good sense I know you have in there somewhere."

Lissie tightened her jaw, fighting rising anger. "I never wanted to see him again."

"I understand." Eunice's tone softened. "But Lissie, he's not the man who walked away from here. From you."

Lissie said nothing.

They were quiet while Lissie poured the hot water, then returned the kettle to the stove. "Menno's matured," Eunice went on. "The boy isn't a boy any longer. He's a man who knows his path, and it's right here with us. With his people."

"So he did become an Englisher," Lissie said, as much to herself as her aunt.

She remembered how badly, as a twenty-year-old, she had wanted to leave the Amish and what she'd seen as their restrictive ways. It wasn't something she wanted anymore. Hadn't for a long time. Even though her life with Alvan hadn't been happy, she'd realized by the time she was in her early twenties that her desire to wear makeup and drive a car had only been a childish fantasy. She was Amish-born and would die Amish. She loved *Gott* and her church and knew that had it not been for her faith, she would never have survived the last ten years.

"*Ya*, an Englisher for a time," Eunice said. She reached to turn up the wick of the old-fashioned glass kerosene lamp in the center of the table. The house had many battery-powered lanterns, but the kerosene lamp was a keepsake—a wedding gift given to Lissie's parents.

Eunice took another cookie from the open tin. "He was an Englisher awhile, then found his way back to Amish in Indiana. New Order." She raised her eyebrows. "But better that than the Englisher Gomorrah he fled. He lived in Indiana for a few years and then one day just showed up on Elizabeth's doorstep."

"And the bishop just let him walk back into a church service?" Lissie asked in amazement. She had always been a little afraid of Phineas Amman, known for his unsmiling face and unyielding insistence that their community stick to the old ways. "After abandoning the church and who knows what else he did?"

Eunice waved her hand dismissively. "Phineas passed a while back. Now we have Bishop Hamul. First, Menno had to confess his sins before the congregation, and so on. He had to meet regularly with the elders." She pulled her teabag from her mug and dumped in spoonfuls of sugar. "But Menno didn't just come back, he returned a better man. And of course, all was forgiven because *Gott* forgives us."

"That He does," Lissie agreed, wishing her mind wasn't racing in so many directions. She had lots of questions, and she couldn't suppress her curiosity. How had

Menno managed to survive in the English world? What kind of work had he done? Where had he lived? Had he bought the red pickup he'd always talked about getting?

"Menno moved home and worked the dairy herd with Jude and his brothers for a bit, but you know how he is. Big ideas. One day, he had a dip of his mother's homemade ice cream and said it was so good he ought to sell it." She slurped her tea. "That's the truth. I was right there under that big silver maple tree of theirs. You know the one. We were making banana splits, but Menno? Oh no. Says his mother's ice cream is the best there is, and he sits there and eats a bowl of nothing but vanilla ice cream the size of his head."

Lissie couldn't resist a smile. She could imagine the family making and eating fancy frozen desserts and Menno sitting there with just his bowl of vanilla.

"Next thing you know," Eunice continued, "he's using milk from Jude's herd and selling ice cream from his mother's office. A woman has an appointment with her midwife and comes home with a half-gallon tub of chocolate chip ice cream. Women these days don't have time for making ice cream, not like they did in my day. Now she has to run the house and the farm so her husband can make a living as a bricklayer or working construction. Anyway, Menno made so much money that he built a shop right here on the main road. Englishers come from miles around to stand in line for Bontrager's ice cream."

As much as she tried to fight it, Lissie couldn't help but be amazed by Menno's success. She was also curious about how a man figured out how to transform a simple homemade recipe into a business. "Did Elizabeth teach him how to make ice cream?" she asked. "I can't imagine she'd have time with her patients, the house, and little

Junia to care for on her own after Boaz died." She hesitated. "But I suppose Junia isn't so little anymore, is she? She's got to be, what, eleven now?" Junia was Menno's youngest sister, while his oldest sister, Bethany, had married a preacher and lived in Ontario, Canada.

"*Ya*, Junia's growing like a weed. A nice girl. Spirited like her mother. Already saying she wants to be a midwife, but we'll see about that. The new bishop, Hamul Weaver, he's a man who wants to look back, not forward."

Lissie leaned back in her chair, sipping her tea. "So… what made Menno leave the Englishers?" When her aunt didn't answer, she leaned forward. "Come on. Something must have happened for him to end up with the Amish again."

"Something must have," Eunice agreed. Her gray eyes twinkled behind the lenses of her eyeglasses. "Guess you'll have to ask him what that something was."

Lissie slapped her hand on the table. "I'll do no such thing. What do I care? I'm done with Menno. Long done. I'm just curious is all," she added with a shrug.

"Not my tale to tell," Eunice said firmly. Her gaze fixed on the clock on the wall, which had been ticking loudly in her mother's kitchen for as long as Lissie could remember. "Time for me to be abed," her aunt announced, rising.

"Anything I can do?"

"To get me ready for bed?" Eunice scoffed. "I've been putting myself to bed for more than twice as long as you've been alive. I might be slow, but I can still get myself under the counterpane." She reached out and caressed Lissie's cheek. "But you can clear the dishes." She headed for the hallway. "And I'll see you and those two bright little pennies in the morning. *Guden nacht*."

Lissie watched her walk down the dark hallway, then

returned to the table to tidy up. Once the mugs were clean and in the dish rack, and the cookie tin was put back in the cupboard, she stood in the middle of the kitchen, unsure what to do. She was exhausted from the overnight bus trip and the emotional turmoil of seeing Menno again. Yet, at the same time, she felt restless. She couldn't stop thinking about how Menno's dream had come true. He'd become an Englisher. But then why had he come back? She couldn't imagine what could have brought him home.

Thinking she could use a little fresh air, she turned down the kerosene lamp on the table and walked out onto the back porch. She breathed deeply of the cool air that carried the scent of lilacs, freshly cut grass and everything that reminded her of home. As her shoulders relaxed, she closed her eyes, listening to the cluck of chickens in the henhouse and the clicking of night insects.

Ohio had never felt this good—never felt this safe.

Lissie sighed and opened her eyes. She needed to go to bed. The children had gone to sleep so early that she knew they'd be up by dawn, and she wanted to be awake for them on their first morning here. But a shower was in order before she slept.

As Lissie turned to go into the house, the distinct sound of a horse and wagon caught her attention. Was that a horse and buggy? Maybe it was out on the road. *Nay*, someone was definitely coming up the driveway. But who would be coming this time of night? It was after nine.

She leaned on the porch rail and watched as two lamplights grew closer. It was a wagon, not a buggy. She could tell by the position of the battery-powered headlights.

As the wagon neared her, Lissie caught a glimpse of the driver. She knew at once who it was.

Menno? What was he doing here this time of night? Surely he didn't think she was going to talk to him.

Angry, Lissie hurried down the porch steps, determined to waylay him before he tied up to the hitching rail. "What do you think you're doing here?" she asked angrily. "I have no intention of talking to you, Menno Bontrager. I didn't want to talk to you today and I don't want to talk to you now!"

The buggy rolled to a stop in front of her. He was smiling, which made her angrier.

"Lissie, I wasn't—"

She interrupted him before he could go on because she had no interest in what he had to say—about anything. "I can't believe you come here this time of night. You've got a lot of nerve, Menno."

"Lissie, I'm not here to talk to you. I'm headed home." He pointed into the darkness ahead.

"Home?" She glanced in the direction he indicated. The *dawdi* house? Eunice was letting him live on her property? Anger rose in her chest. "You live here?" she demanded. "How did—"

A sound came from the wagon's back seat and Lissie turned in surprise. Who was with him?

"*Dat*?" a sleepy voice said. "Are we home, *Dat*?"

Menno looked over his shoulder as a small figure appeared from the shadows on the back bench. "*Ya*, we're home, *dochtur*."

Daughter.

Menno had a daughter?

Chapter Four

Menno groaned and stood as he looked at Lissie. She couldn't have walked out onto the porch at a more inopportune moment. How could this be happening?

He had spent the past year planning the day he would see her again. Not only had he rehearsed everything he wanted to say to her, but he'd also worked hard to make the property look good, painting the houses, barn and outbuildings, seeding the lawn and planting flower beds. Yet nothing today had gone as he'd hoped, and none of his preparation mattered now.

This was not how he wanted her to find out about Daisy. He had wanted to tell Lissie about his daughter before they met, rather than springing the information on her. But after the disaster of being late for Lissie's arrival and her refusal to speak to him, he'd given up on having that conversation today. He'd mentally regrouped and decided it would be best if he and Lissie got a good night's sleep and then could talk. Tomorrow or the next day. He'd had no intention of seeing her again today and certainly not with Daisy in tow.

Menno wiped the back of his hand across his mouth, unsure what to say or do now.

What were the chances Lissie would be standing on the

back porch at the exact moment he arrived? And Daisy was usually such a heavy sleeper. His mother teased that a herd of cows running through her bedroom wouldn't wake her. Yet here Daisy was, staring at Lissie.

She looked from him to Lissie standing between the porch and the wagon. His little girl hesitated and then smiled. "Hi, I'm Daisy," she said, sounding drowsy. Her prayer *kapp* was askew, and long wisps of white-blond hair framed her face. "Are you Eunice's niece? She told me her niece was coming."

Lissie glanced at Menno, her fury plain on her face, but it fell away as she turned to Daisy. "Hello there. I'm sorry if I woke you."

Daisy smiled again, this time shyly. "It's *oll recht*. We're home anyway." She pointed toward their neat-as-a-pin *dawdi* house. "And *Dat* says I'm getting too big to carry. He says I'm going to break his back." At that, she giggled. "So I'd have to wake up to walk into the house anyway."

"Ah, I see." Lissie crossed her arms and looked up at him. Waited.

Menno cleared his throat. "Um… I need to get Daisy to bed. She has school in the morning."

"I could stay home from school," his little girl told him mischievously. She climbed over the seat and plopped down beside him. "And help you at the store."

He tugged at the looped string of her prayer *kapp* that hung down her back. "Nice try, but you're going to school." He lifted his gaze to meet Lissie's. "I won't be long. Come over, and we can sit on my porch. *Mam* sent us home with apple crisp. We could have some dessert and talk."

Lissie dropped her hands to her hips. "I don't want to talk to you."

The quaver in her voice tightened his chest with emotion. He felt deep remorse for the pain he had caused her by leaving the state without her. He also regretted that she had impulsively married a man she didn't know due to his hasty decision to leave Faith's Run alone.

"Lissie," he said, his tone gentle. "We have to talk at some point."

She cocked her head thoughtfully. A halo of golden light from the battery-powered lantern on the wagon's side set her face aglow. "*Nay*, we *don't* have to speak. Not ever again."

He groaned, resisting the urge to slap his hand to his forehead, which would only make her angrier with him. *"Lissie."*

She looked at his daughter. "It was nice to meet you, Daisy." Then, without another word, she marched into the house.

Menno watched her until the screen door slapped shut, and then he lowered himself to the wagon seat.

Nine-year-old Daisy laid her hand on his arm. "Is Lissie a friend of yours, too, *Dat*? Eunice said she was."

He wished Eunice hadn't said anything to Daisy about Lissie and wondered what other details she'd given. He cleared his throat. "From a long time ago, but *ya*, she was."

His daughter raised her blond eyebrows. "She doesn't act like it. She sounds like she's mad at you."

Menno threw his head back and laughed, then urged his horse forward, praying that tomorrow would be better.

After dropping Daisy off at school the following morning, Menno poured two cups of black coffee from a large percolator on his mother's stove. He then went through the house and into the waiting room, where his mother's patients relaxed until their names were called. The comfortable room looked more like a parlor than a waiting room in a medical office, and there were already five women seated and another coming in the door from the parking area.

He spotted his mother. Like the other women in the room, she wore a tab dress and organza prayer *kapp*, but she also wore a plain, knee-length white coat over it. She was speaking to a very nervous-looking woman who was listening intently.

"Menno! What a nice surprise!" someone said, startling him.

He whipped around, the coffee sloshing in the mugs. It was Rose Yoder, who worked part-time as a receptionist for the midwifery office.

"Rose." Groaning inwardly, he smiled. He liked her well enough, but the young woman was too flirtatious for his taste. He wasn't opposed to unmarried men and women flirting. Though it differed from what he'd seen among the English, it was also part of the ritual leading to marriage among the Amish. What he opposed was her overt behavior, especially since he'd told her he wasn't interested. When he joined the church in Faith's Run, he made it clear to would-be matchmakers that he was a devoted father with no intention of marrying anytime soon. Still, that didn't stop some girls from trying to catch his attention.

"Oh, is one of those for me?" Rose giggled as she reached for one of the mugs he carried.

He turned so the coffee was out of her reach. "Um… *nay*, sorry. This one is for my *mam*. And I already drank from this one." He raised one and then the other, feeling awkward.

"Oh." She pulled a pile of patient clipboards to her chest and pouted with great exaggeration. "I was hoping you had brought me one. I like my coffee with lots of cream and sugar." She swayed her hips ever-so-slightly, smiling up at him. "If you ever want to bring me one."

He nodded but didn't say anything, fearing it would only encourage her. He never knew what to say to women when they expressed romantic interest in him. There had been no courting in his life since Lissie. His relationship with Daisy's mother had just happened.

"So what's the new special flavor going to be?" Rose asked. She was pretty: blond hair, blue eyes, a nice figure, but he didn't like how she looked at him—like he was a bass in the pond and she was about to scoop him up in her net.

He blinked. "Sorry?"

"Ice cream, silly!" She followed this with another giggle, and one of his neighbors, Tilly Swartzentruber, glanced up at them, then went back to reading a woman's magazine.

Menno eyed his mother. She was still speaking with her patient. "Um...not sure," he told Rose. "Probably strawberry. We've got some nice berries ripening in the greenhouse."

"I love strawberry." Every word she spoke somehow sounded coy. "Maybe my sisters and I will come one day. And you can show me around your shop."

He considered handing her his mother's coffee and making a run for it, but he hadn't seen her this morning yet. His youngest brother, Phineas, had told him a patient had arrived at 3:00 a.m., and Menno thought she might need some caffeine after such an early start.

"Not much to see around the shop," he told Rose. "Just freezers full of ice cream and cases of cones and napkins. We make the ice cream in the new kitchen out back." The moment he added that detail, he regretted it. It was unwise to encourage Rose in any way, or he'd have a hard time getting away from her.

"Rose?" his mother called.

Menno sighed with relief.

"I'd love to see the kitchen too," Rose said, ignoring her boss.

"Rose." His mother repeated, walking over to them. "That's Annie there." She indicated the young woman she'd been speaking to. "She'll need a new patient packet. And I think Tilly and Mary John need to update their records." Her tone wasn't stern, but there was no way to misinterpret it. She wanted Rose to move along.

"Sure." Rose smiled at Menno and then walked away.

His mother accepted the mug of coffee from him as she watched Rose go. "Didn't I hear that she and Jeb Yoder are expected to announce their engagement any time now?" she whispered.

"That's what Asher told me." He sipped his coffee, purposely not looking in Rose's direction.

His mother harrumphed. "She doesn't act like a woman about to plan a wedding."

He smiled into his cup.

"Walk with me?" His *mam* tilted her head toward the closed door leading to a hallway. Off the hallway, there were two examination rooms, two labor suites, a full bath with a shower, a storage closet and her private office. The addition had been built fifteen years ago and had been the talk of the town back then. Some folks believed it was a waste of money. Others deemed it *hockmut*, a prideful show of their midwife's success. But his *dat* had been the one who'd designed the addition. He'd firmly believed in its necessity, even when his wife wavered. His father had insisted it was important for Amish women to have the right to good health care in a place where they felt most comfortable. His mother delivered in homes as well as the cozy suites. Of course, some Amish women had to see Englisher doctors and go to the local hospital, whether out of necessity or preference. His mother's midwife practice gave Amish women choices.

"I didn't want to bother you. Looks like you've got a busy day," he said, as he followed her.

"*Ya*, but I'm never too busy for my children." She threw a look over her shoulder. "Especially for the ones who seem to need more guidance than others."

He felt his face flush, but knew her words came out of love for him, not judgment.

Elizabeth Bontrager was a handsome, fit woman to be reckoned with. In her late fifties, she had curly red hair barely covered by her prayer *kapp*, high cheekbones, freckles and brilliant brown eyes that didn't miss a thing. She never shied away from voicing her opinion, asked or not; her children and their bishop could attest to that.

"I'm sorry I never made it to supper last night," she said as they went through the door to the back. "Nancy Fischer's seventh. A beautiful little girl."

"It's *oll recht*. We know better than to expect you." He followed her into her office. "And Sheba likes thinking she's in charge."

His mother's youthful laughter filled her office. "But I wanted to be here to hear how things went with Lissie." Before he could respond, she said, "Close the door."

For a moment, Menno considered telling her he had to

go, that he had a hundred things to do today. But he knew there was no sense in avoiding her when she wanted to talk because she wouldn't take no for an answer.

His mother dropped into a leather swivel chair behind a massive oak desk. "Junia said things didn't go well."

He knitted his brows. His eleven-year-old sister, born days after his father's death, was already becoming a woman to be reckoned with, just like her mother. And she was as nosy as their grandmother, Sheba. "Junia? She wasn't even there."

His mother frowned. "She said Lissie walked all the way home rather than ride in the same wagon with you."

"My *grossmammi* doesn't have to tell everything she knows." He drank from his mug. "And Lissie didn't walk all the way home," he added defensively.

His *mam*'s steady gaze held his. "You know I always liked Lissie, but are you sure you want to pursue this?"

"Absolutely." He took a step closer to her desk. "*Mam*, you of all people know what it means to love someone. I thought I lost her forever. And then…" He blew out his breath. "When I heard that her husband passed, I just knew—I knew this is what *Gott* intended for me. That Lissie is intended for me. And I for her."

"And what of Daisy?"

He gestured with his free hand. "She needs a mother. You've said so yourself. And Daisy thinks I need a wife. I told you she tried to get me to give Jack Yoder's granddaughter a ride home last Sunday after church. The one visiting from Lancaster."

She smiled. "Your *dochtur*'s growing up. She wants what's best for you." She sobered. "We all do. Your siblings, your grandmother, Eunice. Me."

"And I appreciate that, *Mam*. But this is my life and I

intend to make my own decisions. My own mistakes, if that's how it all turns out." He hesitated. "I'm doing pretty well making mistakes with Lissie already."

"How's that?"

He fiddled with one of his leather suspenders. "I didn't get to tell her about Daisy. How could I? She wouldn't talk to me."

"Hard to talk with her walking and you riding," her mother said, trying to lighten the mood.

She got half a smile out of him, then he said, "She found out before I could tell her."

His mother looked surprised. "Junia didn't tell me that."

"Only because she didn't know. It happened last night, after supper here. Daisy and I were going up our driveway and—"

"Lissie saw you. Saw Daisy."

"It was dark," he bemoaned. "And getting on to bedtime. I figured Lissie would be asleep after such a long day. With her taking an overnight bus and all. Having her two little ones and no one to help her." He glanced up sheepishly. "But *ya*, there she was on the porch. And Daisy, she's asleep in the back, so I think I'm going to sneak her past Lissie, but—"

"But there's no sneaking anything past Lissie Shetler," she finished for him, amusement still in her voice.

He shook his head slowly. "*Nay*, there is not. Lissie saw her."

"And how did she take it?"

He gave his mother a look that said everything without saying a word.

"Not so happy, I suppose," she murmured.

"Not so happy. Not with me, not with Daisy. Lissie

was as sweet as she could be to Daisy. She was all Daisy talked about on the way to school this morning. She's eager to meet Lissie's Naomi and Jonah. Eunice told her that she and Naomi are close in age. Daisy's sure that they're going to be the best of friends."

His mother took a sip of coffee. "And I pray they will be."

Menno sighed. "Speaking of Daisy, I told her she was staying here tonight. I hope that's *oll recht*. I don't know what will happen yet, and I was thinking…maybe I should give Lissie a day or so to cool down." He hesitated and then went on. "But if she doesn't—if she does something crazy like get back on a bus to Ohio, I don't want Daisy to be any more disappointed than she'll already be."

"You don't want Daisy making friends with Naomi if they won't be staying?"

He frowned. "Is that terrible?"

"It's practical, and it's what parents do. We try to protect our children—even our adult children. Which is why I'm nosing into your business."

"*Mam*, I don't need your protection."

"I know," she said gently. "But you'll see someday. It doesn't matter how old your *kinner* are, they're still your little ones in your heart." They were both quiet for a moment, lost in their thoughts, and then she leaned forward, arms on her desk. "*Oll recht*, so you're going to do this. I'm here for you. Is there anything I can do to help?"

He rested his hand on the doorknob. He needed to get to work. He shrugged. "Be nice to her. Welcome her. I don't know all the details, but Sheba says she's not had an easy life. Especially since she lost her husband. I don't think her in-laws have been kind to her. She's been dependent on them since the husband died."

"Happens more often than you realize, *sohn*. And not just far from Kent County. I hear a lot of things from my patients. Everyone likes to think the Amish are perfect. But we have the same problems Englishers do. Alcohol, drugs, suicide, mental illness."

"I know firsthand," he admitted soberly. While Daisy's mother had never been diagnosed, thinking back, Menno knew that she'd suffered from some sort of psychological problem. Heather went through cycles where she either went a mile a minute or couldn't get out of bed.

"It's going to be all right, Menno. No matter what happens with Lissie." His *mam* smiled at him, and even at twenty-nine and a parent himself, her approval warmed his heart. "I should let you start your office hours. Maybe I'll see you at supper."

"Maybe," she agreed, picking up a chart from a pile on her desk.

"Have a good day," he said as he entered the hall.

She didn't look up from her desk. "And you. Love you, *sohn*."

"Love you, too." Menno closed the door and paused for a moment. When he woke up that morning, a thread of doubt still lingered in his heart—doubt that God intended him to marry Lissie. However, knowing that his mother and his entire family stood behind him reinforced that with their support and God's greater plan, he'd be married by fall.

Chapter Five

The next morning, Lissie woke to bright sunlight streaming across the patchwork quilt on her parents' bed. Realizing she must have overslept, she sprang upright. How could that be? She always rose before dawn, whether it was summer or winter. She'd been a hard worker since she was a girl, never shying away from her responsibilities as a daughter and, later, as a wife and mother. There were too many things to get done in a day to laze about like this. She swung her feet onto the handmade rag rug and straightened the rumpled sheets.

Of course, it was understandable that she overslept. After her encounter with Menno, she'd gone straight to bed, but although exhausted, she hadn't been able to fall asleep. Instead, she'd tossed and turned for hours, thinking of all the ways she should have told him off.

Lissie couldn't believe Menno was living on the property. Why? How had that happened? What was even more upsetting, or perhaps *startling* was a better word, was that he was a father. She couldn't believe her aunt hadn't mentioned any of this before Lissie uprooted her children and took them from the only place they'd ever known. Lissie knew that Menno had become an Englisher just as he'd planned. *They* had planned. When had he become Amish again? Was he married? Widowed? Were there other children? With so many unanswered questions swirling in her mind, it was a wonder she'd managed to sleep at all.

Trying to push Menno from her mind, Lissie looked for a clock. Her parents had kept a wind-up one on the dresser. Sure enough, there it was, as if nothing had changed since she left the house ten years ago. She blinked, staring at the white hands on the plain black face. Seven o'clock? She'd usually have been up for hours by this time. Why hadn't she seen or heard from her *kinner*? Had Naomi and Jonah slept in too? That seemed even more unlikely than her oversleeping, but where were they if they were awake? They would have come to her room if they'd woken before her, wouldn't they? Fighting a wave of panic, she rummaged through her suitcase on the floor, pulling out clean clothes.

What kind of mother was she that she'd lain abed while leaving her children to wake up in a strange house? She put on her dress. Where had she placed the straight pins for her bodice when she had removed them last night while getting ready for bed?

Buttons were against the *Ordnung*, the rules and regulations the Amish followed. However, as the English world changed, many Old Order Amish had relaxed some rules, especially personal ones that made life more challenging. Nowadays, most Amish women wore sneakers and pinned their dresses closed with safety pins. But not in her husband's home; he had not been swayed by the modern trapping of Englishers. He had made that clear to her within days of their doomed marriage. The rules became even stricter when they were forced to move in with his parents after being evicted from their home due to unpaid rent.

Lissie spotted her straight pins on the dresser next to the clock and rushed to retrieve them. She pushed the first one through the thinning fabric of her bodice and pricked herself. "Ow," she muttered, bringing her finger, with its single drop of blood, to her mouth. As she reached for another pin, she silently vowed that once she had her own money, the first thing she would buy would be a whole card of safety pins. Then she and Naomi would relegate all the straight pins to the sewing basket and never poke themselves while getting dressed again.

Lissie's son's laughter drifted through the wide oak floorboards from downstairs, and she lifted her head to listen. Naomi's giggles followed, and Lissie took a deep breath, forcing herself to calm down. *There's no need to worry*, she told herself. *The children are fine. We're safe. We're far from my in-laws and back home in Faith's Run.*

From downstairs, Lissie heard her aunt's voice, and even though she was angry that she hadn't told her about Menno, she couldn't help but smile. She had missed Eunice, who had been more of a mother to her than her own. However, her mood darkened as she returned to the full gravity of the situation she had put herself and her children in. Had she been too impulsive in deciding to return? Should she have questioned her aunt further before leaving her in-laws' house? Because, yes, she was home. But so was Menno. And this little berg wasn't big enough for both of them. She wasn't even sure the state of Delaware was big enough.

Dressed in her only other weekday dress, one even shabbier than the one she'd worn yesterday, Lissie pulled through her suitcase looking for her hairbrush. What was she going to do now? Return to Ohio? Could she do that to her children? What were her other options if she wasn't going to stay here?

Should they go to Tennessee, where her oldest brother and his family lived? She knew Mahlon would let them stay with him, but they were practically strangers. Mahlon was twenty-five years older than Lissie. Plus, her brother already had a full house. He had his in-laws to care for, along with his children, who still lived at home. According to Eunice, they didn't even have a real house. Mahlon had built a small pole barn with just the essentials to live there until he could construct a proper home.

Lissie ran her hairbrush through her thick, curly brown hair. She twisted and pinned it up, covering it with a navy blue kerchief tied at her nape. Once suitably dressed, she left the bedroom and hurried downstairs.

"*Mam*!" Naomi called as Lissie padded barefoot into the kitchen.

The cheerful greeting from her typically serious daughter made Lissie smile. Her children were seated at the kitchen table, which was heavily laden with breakfast foods. There were pancakes, scrambled eggs, scrapple, bacon, buttermilk biscuits, a block of butter, and jars of jam and jelly.

"*Endie* let me help make pancakes, *Mam*," Naomi announced proudly. "You never let me help cook."

Because your grandmother wouldn't allow it. Nor would your dat, Lissie thought. Too much mess, they had insisted.

"Want to see?" Naomi pointed at the serving platter in front of her with her fork. "Animal pancakes." She frowned, tilting her head, first one way and then the other. Her daughter wore the same dress as the previous day, but her prayer *kapp* had been replaced by a black kerchief. "Well, they're supposed to look like animals. Mine aren't very good."

"Nonsense," Eunice declared, coming out of the walk-in pantry on the far side of the room. With a jar of canned peaches in her hand, she came to the table to study Naomi's handiwork. "I can see that's a pig plain as day. And there's a cat."

Naomi looked at her great-aunt as earnestly as a nine-year-old could muster. "*Endie*, they're supposed to be chickens and goats!"

Eunice cackled and went to the counter to set the peaches down. "They still taste good."

"They must," Lissie agreed, watching her son thrust a forkful—dripping in maple syrup—into his mouth. "Jonah sure likes them." She tousled his dark, silky mop of hair. Both children looked like her, with no similarities to their father's pale skin and hair.

Eunice glanced at Lissie, pulled a church key from a drawer and opened the canning jar. "Sleep well your first night home?"

Lissie crossed her arms. "I didn't." She took care to temper her tone. "Not after running into Menno outside after you went to bed."

Her aunt drew back, looking shocked. "What were you doing outside? The house was all buttoned up when I left you. I thought you were off to bed, too."

Lissie eyed her. It was just like Eunice to avoid the point if she didn't like it. "I was on the porch getting some air when Menno arrived and told me he lives here."

Eunice dumped the sliced peaches in silky syrup into a serving bowl. "He doesn't live here. He lives in the *dawdi haus*." She brought the peaches to the table.

"And he had someone with him. A little girl?"

"Ja." Eunice grinned. "Daisy."

"We need to talk," Lissie said, her tone not disrespectful but firm.

Eunice sighed, pulled out her chair and plopped down. "But first we eat." She adjusted her wire-frame eyeglasses and met Lissie's gaze. "We'll have breakfast, and then we send these two rascals—" she poked Jonah in the ribs and he giggled "—to collect eggs while we clean up."

Lissie was silent for a moment. She didn't want to wait until later to talk to her aunt about the mess she'd gotten herself into. She wanted to discuss it now, while she was feeling good and angry. But then she looked at her children seated on the same bench Lissie had sat on as a child, and her resolve crumbled. They seemed happier than she could remember seeing them in ages. And the food looked amazing. There had never been such abundance in her husband's home, and certainly not in his parents'. Sometimes, it had been due to a lack of money with her and Alvan, but with her in-laws, it was simply because they were stingy.

And maybe they shouldn't talk about Menno in front of Naomi and Jonah. What if Eunice let slip their mother's previous relationship with him? Lissie's stomach grumbled, and she pressed her hand to her belly.

"Come on," Eunice coaxed. She scooped peaches into a small bowl and set it at the place setting already prepared for her. "Eat, and then we'll talk, Lissie. A person can always reason better on a full stomach."

Lissie placed her hand on the back of the chair in which her father had sat throughout her life in his home.

"Naomi and I made the scrapple crispy, just the way you like it," Eunice said in a sing-song voice.

Lissie pulled out the chair and sat down. "Fine," she

conceded as she reached for the platter of pancakes. "But after breakfast, you and I will have that talk."

"*Ya*, *ya*, *ya*," Eunice agreed. Then she stuffed a forkful of peaches into her mouth, her eyes twinkling triumphantly.

Eunice thought she had won, but Lissie hoped her aunt knew better. They would have that conversation, but for now, Lissie yielded and enjoyed the best breakfast she'd had in years.

Forty minutes later, Lissie urged her children out the back door with a basket, reminding them how to collect eggs from a nest without bothering the hens. They didn't have much experience with chickens; her husband's family preferred buying eggs from large retailers. Nonetheless, there had been a run-down chicken house at several rental homes over the years, and Lissie had managed to keep a few hens.

"Keep an eye on him," Lissie warned Naomi, pointing at Jonah.

"Can we go see the goats?" Jonah asked.

Lissie placed his flat-brimmed straw hat on his head. "*Ya*, but listen to your sister. And don't go into the pasture." She watched them cross the porch, a bounce in their steps. She smiled, but it faded as soon as she closed the screen door behind them and returned to the kitchen.

"Why didn't you tell me Menno lived here?" Lissie asked Eunice. The older woman was busy scraping the plates into a stainless-steel container where clean food scraps were collected to feed the chickens. "Why didn't you tell me he was in Faith's Run?" Lissie continued speaking faster than before. "That he was Amish. That he had a daughter?" Her last words caught in her throat.

She was hurt but mostly just angry. "How could you do this to me, *Endie*?"

Eunice crossed her arms. "You done now with your little temper fit?"

Lissie lowered her gaze, embarrassed by her outburst. "I'm sorry. That was disrespectful, especially after all you've done for me." Her aunt had not only opened her home to Lissie and her *kinner* but also had sent her the money for the bus tickets to get here. It was wrong not to be more grateful. Who else in the world would have done this for her? Certainly not any of her siblings. If she were going to move to Tennessee, she'd have to find a job to earn enough money for train or bus tickets to get there.

Eunice washed her hands, went to the stove and turned on the kettle. "Sit."

"*Nay*, I need to help you clean up." Lissie picked up the bowl of leftover peaches. "You should be the one sitting."

Eunice met Lissie halfway to the sink. "Respect your elders. Sit. I'm making coffee. You still like coffee, don't you?"

Lissie nodded as her aunt took the bowl from her.

"The dishes can wait. I never knew a dirty dish that got up and walked anywhere," Eunice said. "We'll have coffee, you and me. I only got the one cup before those rapscallions came down this morning."

"I'm sorry," Lissie said. "I should have told them to stay upstairs and wait for me if they woke first. They shouldn't have bothered you. I was expecting them to sleep—"

"Now you're being ridiculous." Eunice sounded annoyed. "You know how long it's been since there were children in this house? Put another five years on my life just seeing those two come racing down this morning."

She grinned. “Did my heart good. Old folks like me, we need young ones.” She hesitated, then pointed to the chair. “Sit.”

So Lissie did as she was told and waited until they both had full cups of coffee in front of them. It felt strange to Lissie to see dirty dishes on the table and the counter. This would never happen in the Alvan Shetler household.

“So…why didn’t I tell you Menno moved back three years ago?” Eunice asked. She spun a wooden spoon in a small blue, crockery honey pot and watched a long string of sweetness fall into her coffee. “Because, like I said, you’d never have come.”

Lissie eyed her over her mug of black coffee.

“Which would have been a mistake,” Eunice added. “You needed to get out of Ohio, away from those terrible people.”

“They weren’t—”

“Hush now,” Eunice cut in. “I’m talking. And I have a right to my own opinion.” She poured heavy cream into her coffee, stirred, tasted it with a loud slurp and added more. “Those Shetlers were a bad bunch. Knew it when I met them at your wedding, and you’re well to be rid of them. Not all Amish are good people. Every apple basket’s got a rotten one in it.”

Lissie sighed. She didn’t want to talk about her husband and in-laws’ shortcomings; she’d lived with their failings for ten years. But that part of her life was over. She was here now, and the present was what she needed to focus on—along with her and her children’s futures. “Let’s forget about Alvan for now. Tell me why Menno’s living here,” she said, wrapping her fingers around the warm mug. “On this property.”

“Ah, that. *Ya*.” Eunice sat back in her chair. “It all

started when your brother Mahlon left Faith's Run after your father and mother had passed, what, six years ago? Seven?"

"Seven," Lissie confirmed. "I'd just had Jonah and was in the hospital when *Dat* died." Her little boy had been born prematurely, and the delivery had been difficult. She hadn't been able to travel to Delaware for her father's funeral. Not her mother's either, because she'd just had Naomi. That was the sad reality of living far from family. She'd learned that the hard way, along with many other tough lessons related to her isolation from those she loved and who loved her.

"Whelp," Eunice continued, "Mahlon packed up his wife and children and off they went."

"And you didn't want to move. I remember you saying that in a letter you wrote to me."

"*Nay*, I wasn't going. That Mahlon and I, we never got along. Like oil and water, the two of us." She frowned. "And I wasn't going to leave Sheba to traipse off to Tennessee," she added indignantly. "She's a sister to me."

Lissie smiled faintly as she listened. She knew how close Menno's grandmother and her aunt were. They'd been best friends for decades. "*Oll recht*," she said, pressing forward. "Mahlon and his family went to Tennessee. How does that put Menno in our *dawdi haus*?"

Eunice tilted her head dramatically from side to side as she spoke. "Mahlon, see, he couldn't sell the farm because no one would pay him what he wanted for it. The boy isn't right. He was asking way more than it was worth and the place wasn't in good shape—broken windmill, shutters hanging, hole in the barn roof." She snorted. "When he couldn't sell it, he rented it out. I don't know how many families came and went. Four? Five? Some stayed less than a year."

"*Ya*, I knew he had rented it," Lissie said, "but I assumed that was because he wanted to keep it. In case Tennessee wasn't what he was hoping it would be." She set her coffee on the table. "But you told me you were in the *dawdi haus* and the renters lived here." She studied her aunt, trying to work it all out in her head. "Then, around last Thanksgiving—Alvan had already passed—you wrote to me that you moved back into the big house. I remember asking more than once why you were here again, but you never said."

Eunice's eyes widened behind her glasses. "I couldn't very well tell you that Menno bought the whole place, could I?"

Anger flushed her face, and Lissie pressed her lips together to keep herself from saying something she would regret. She realized how convenient her lack of access to a telephone made it for her aunt to devise this scheme to bring her back here without knowing anything about Menno. She couldn't help but be impressed that her octogenarian aunt had managed to pull it off.

"Menno bought my parents' farm?" Lissie asked, carefully keeping her voice even.

"*Mahlon's* farm," Eunice corrected. "*Gott* knows I loved my big brother, but he was a fool when it came to his children. I told him he ought to leave this place to you, that you'd take care of the whole family. But of course that wasn't something your *dat* would do."

"Because boys inherit, not girls." Lissie mused, lifting her hand to her forehead. Her thoughts were going in so many directions that she struggled to focus. "So Menno bought the farm," she repeated. "Did he pay my brother what he was asking?" She didn't know why she cared.

Eunice slurped her coffee. "Menno never said what he gave for the place, but I imagine he did. I told you Menno Bontrager has done well for himself."

Lissie thought about the timeline and frowned as she mulled over the details. Menno had purchased the farm *after* Alvan's death. Surely her aunt hadn't intended for her and the children to come here so that Lissie and Menno would get back together. The idea was absurd. "Was this all your idea, Menno buying our place?" she demanded, her anger flaring again.

"My idea?" Eunice drew back as if offended, which made Lissie all the more suspicious. "Certainly not. You know Elizabeth's boys. Minds of their own. The boy built a nice business for himself, and he wanted his own place."

Lissie didn't know what to say. She was angry and hurt that her aunt had manipulated her like this. Surely, Eunice hadn't thought Menno could just walk back into Lissie's life after he'd devastated it.

Lissie sat back in the chair, crossing her arms. Did she ask Eunice to buy her bus tickets and take Naomi and Jonah back to Alvan's parents? At least until she could figure out her next step. It might take some convincing, but maybe her brother would let them move in temporarily. She closed her eyes. The thought of returning to the Shetlers' house made her stomach turn.

A sound drifted in from an open window, and Lissie opened her eyes. It was laughter—Naomi and Jonah were laughing. Her heart swelled with joy. Children were meant to laugh, and her *kinner* hadn't laughed enough. Maybe she could endure her in-laws' unkindness again, but upon hearing that sweet sound of her children's delight, she knew she couldn't put them through it again—not ever.

Returning to Ohio was not an option for her; that would be impulsive and selfish. They would have to relocate to Tennessee if she wanted to leave Faith's Run to escape from Menno. And that would require money; Lissie needed to find a job. She took a deep breath and reached for her coffee. In the meantime, she would do her best to avoid Menno. And when she couldn't, as a good Christian woman, she saw no reason why she couldn't get along with him as a neighbor.

Chapter Six

After a boisterous supper with his brothers, sister, mother and grandmother, Menno remained at the house until sunset, playing games on the back porch. He was tired and would have preferred to skip Friday game night, but he stayed to avoid returning home and the risk of facing Lissie unprepared again. All day, he had been pondering his next move with her. How did he begin with her again after the rocky start to the new relationship he desperately wanted? He needed to talk to her, of course. But should he give her time to adjust to them living on the same property before having that conversation? Or should he knock on her door and insist on talking with her now? Knowing how stubborn she could be, if he didn't initiate their next conversation, it might be weeks before she said so much as a *guder mariye* to him. He was still considering the possibilities when he gave his daughter a hug good-night and headed home alone.

As he drove his wagon the short distance between the farms, Menno prayed to *Gott* for help with his dilemma. He'd had Lissie's love and then abandoned her like he'd left his flat-brimmed church hat on his bed when he said goodbye to his Amish life. So many times, he'd contemplated how his and Lissie's lives would have been different if he had stayed in Faith's Run or taken her with him. But what was done was done; now he needed to live in the present.

As he crept up the shared driveway, hoping to avoid drawing attention, he spotted Eunice standing on her back porch. She seemed to be waiting. For him? He wouldn't put it past the clever old fox. She and his grandmother were as alike as two peas in a pod. They enjoyed meddling, but he didn't see their nosiness as genuine interfering so much as maneuvering with good intentions.

He pulled back on the reins and glanced upward at the house as the wagon stopped. Lights glowed in several upstairs windows, and he assumed Lissie was putting her children to bed. He pictured her on her knees, praying at her daughter's bedside the way he and Daisy prayed each night. Was there a chance he and Lissie might one day do that together?

He watched as Eunice hurried down the steps. She could be spry for a woman her age when she wanted to be.

"Were you waiting for me?" he asked.

She came over to lean on the side of his buckboard wagon. "No Daisy?" Eunice was good at avoidance when it suited her.

"She stayed over. She, *Mam* and Junia have plans to make cookies and start flower seedlings in the morning." Junia was his eleven-year-old sister, born after their *dat* died of a heart attack.

"It's nice that Daisy spends time with her *grossmammi*, *gross-grossmammi* and *endie*," Eunice said, looking at him like she knew there was more to his explanation.

He sighed, "Truth be told, I needed some time to myself."

Eunice nodded, understanding without judgment in

her eyes. It was one of the reasons he liked her so much. Loved her, in fact. She often gave him her opinion when he didn't ask for it, but she was also supportive in ways his mother and siblings couldn't be. Eunice was his friend.

Menno exhaled in a sigh and went on. "I… I waited so long for her." He stared at the flower beds in the shadows of the porch he'd so tenderly prepared for Lissie's homecoming. "And then I made a mess of things."

"You didn't. Seeing you again was a shock is all. You need to give her some time and grace. And give yourself grace, Menno. And trust that whatever unfolds is *Gott*'s will."

"I feel guilty that we didn't tell her I was here. How do we know this is *Gott*'s will and not yours and mine?"

She shrugged. "We don't. Not yet, at least. We pray and we wait. What will be will be." She lifted her hands off his wagon. "I'm off to bed. I was watching for you because I wanted to invite you and Daisy for supper tomorrow night."

He raised an eyebrow. "To supper? Here? With you and Lissie and the children?"

Eunice bobbed her head. "*Ya*, it's what I said."

"And you don't think it's too soon?"

She cackled. "Guess we'll see, won't we?"

He tilted his head, studying her. He wanted nothing more than to sit across from Lissie at the supper table. They didn't even have to talk; he just wanted to gaze at her beautiful face and hear her voice. In fact, *not* talking seemed like a good idea after their last conversations. "Does Lissie know you're inviting me?"

"Just because my niece is here doesn't mean you and Daisy and I can't keep sharing supper. The nights you two come are my favorite days of the week."

Not an answer.

He glanced away. It was a bad idea, he thought. *Too soon. Too much.*

"Please, Menno?" Eunice's tone softened, and for a moment, she sounded her age. "Do this for me? I want this for you. For Lissie. The two of you deserve to be happy."

"She's going to be so angry when she finds out we've been planning this for nearly a year."

"Let her be. Once she realizes she's still in love with you, she'll come around," Eunice said. "In the meantime, come for supper. When you knit a blanket, you have to start somewhere."

He exhaled loudly. When she used her little-old-lady tone, she knew he couldn't say no to her. "*Ya*, we'll come."

Eunice clasped her hands together and grinned. "*Goot.* See you tomorrow, then."

Menno watched her walk into the house and urged his horse forward, hoping he wouldn't regret this.

Usually, Menno and Daisy walked into Eunice's house without knocking. They moved between each other's homes as if they were family, because they had become family. The next day, however, when Daisy started to open the screen door leading from the back porch into the mudroom, he placed his hand on her shoulder, stopping her. "It's not just Eunice living here anymore," he whispered in her ear. "Lissie's here, too. Remember?"

"And Naomi!" Daisy's blue eyes were wide and filled with excitement.

"*Ya*, Naomi, too." He hadn't talked much with Daisy about Lissie's *kinner*, especially the girl, because he didn't want to get Daisy's hopes up. His daughter didn't like being an only child and desperately wanted a best friend.

He wanted Naomi to be more than a friend to her. He wanted them to be sisters, but they were a long way from that right now.

"Knocking is the polite thing to do," he explained quietly. "They don't know us like Eunice does. It would be like…like walking into our new preacher's house without knocking."

She wrinkled her nose. "Why would we want to walk into *his* house? He smells like mothballs and he spits when he talks. You can see his spittle when he preaches Sunday mornings."

It was all Menno could do not to laugh out loud. She wasn't wrong, but this was neither the time nor the place to address being too honest. Instead, he drew her back and knocked on the door. "*Hallo*!" he called.

He heard footsteps, but they weren't Eunice's, and for a moment, he had the urge to run. But then it was too late.

Lissie appeared and their gazes met through the screen door. He immediately recognized anger in her brown eyes. "What are you doing here?" she whispered, but her tone demanded an answer. Then she saw Daisy behind him, and the corners of her mouth lifted into the faintest smile. "*Hallo* there."

Daisy moved in front of Menno. "We're here for supper."

"Are you, now?" Lissie looked at him again. She was still smiling, but it was clear her smile wasn't for him.

Menno *knew* this was a bad idea. Why had he agreed to come? "Um, Eunice invited us," he explained.

"For supper," Daisy chimed in. "We brought ice cream from *Daddi*'s shop." She held up a black-and-white cooler bag.

"Eunice invited you?" Lissie stared at him with hostility. But then she stepped back and opened the door. "Then I guess you best come in."

The next hour was one of the most painful that Menno had spent in a long time. Eunice and Lissie had prepared an amazing spread of fried chicken, slippery dumplings, mashed potatoes, garlic green beans and buttermilk biscuits. He ate heartily because he was hungry, but observed, rather than participated, in the evening's banter. Not only did Lissie shift down a seat to avoid sitting across from him, but she also refused to speak to him beyond *please* and *thank you*.

Lissie's sweetness toward Daisy was the only thing that saved supper from being a complete disaster. She chatted with her without asking prying questions, making Daisy beam as she soaked up the attention. Naomi was equally kind. By the time supper was over, the two girls were making plans to go cut lilac blooms before it got dark.

As Lissie and Eunice cleared the table, Menno stacked Daisy's plate on top of his, debating whether he should help with the cleanup. Men carried their dishes to the sink in his mother's house because she had raised four boys. However, before he could decide, Eunice decided for him.

"I have an idea," she announced loudly. "Menno—" she eyed him "—why don't you and Lissie take a walk and catch up?"

Without meaning to do it, he instinctively looked at Lissie. She seemed more startled than him. He gulped. "A walk?"

Lissie tore her gaze from Menno's. "*A walk*?" she repeated.

"Ya." Eunice took the plates from his hands and passed them to Daisy. "It's been years since you've seen each

other, and I know you're eager to catch up. The children and I can *rett* this kitchen."

Although the suggestion took him by surprise, he appreciated Eunice's encouragement. For months, he had been having conversations with Lissie in his mind. He had so much to share about his life since they parted, and he wanted to learn about hers, both the good and the bad. He also wanted to express his regret for leaving the way he had.

Lissie glanced at him. "You've probably got better things to do than go for a walk. Chores?" she suggested.

He shook his head slowly. "*Nay*, no chores. Daisy and I fed the horses and the goats when we got home earlier from *Mam*'s." He tilted his head toward the back door. "Let's take a walk."

He watched Lissie clench her hands at her sides and then release them. She glanced at her children, whom Eunice was enlisting to help. The two girls huddled together, giggling as they stacked dishes. Eunice had given Jonah a bottle of dish soap and he stood on a stool, making bubbles in the clean water.

"Please, Lissie," Menno murmured. "You can't avoid me forever."

"I can't?" she asked, some of the fight gone from her voice. He saw resignation on her face.

"*Nay*, you can't. I won't let you," he told her.

She sighed, and her shoulders slumped. Her dress looked like it had seen better days, but it didn't make her any less beautiful. She had a kerchief over her head, and curly tendrils that had escaped her bun framed her face. His hand itched to touch one like he had when they'd been walking out together.

"I won't be long," Lissie stated flatly.

"Take your time." Eunice grinned. "We'll have ice cream when you get back. Daisy said you brought my favorite—rocky road with lots of marshmallows!"

In the mudroom, Menno opened the back door and then halted. "You want shoes?" he asked Lissie. He indicated her bare feet.

She walked past him. "We won't be going far."

Her tone made him wonder once more if this was a bad idea. What was the point of forcing it if she didn't want to talk to him? On the other hand, what if he didn't get another chance to talk to her alone—*ever*? He prayed that wouldn't be the case, but he needed to tell her he was sorry for hurting her all those years ago and couldn't let this opportunity slip away.

He allowed her to take the lead as they silently walked through the barnyard. Before he realized where she was heading, they found themselves on a path leading to the pond her father had dug when they were children. It had been stocked with bass, and he and Lissie had spent countless hours fishing there, first as childhood friends and later while dating.

The path he kept mowed widened, and he fell into step beside her. Realizing he needed to be the one to speak first, he took a deep breath. "Thank you for doing this. I wanted to talk to you, but not within earshot of the children. I need to apologize to you, Lissie, for leaving you behind after we made plans together."

She said nothing and he glanced at a patch of milkweed along the path. A monarch butterfly lifted off a leaf and fluttered in front of them in the warm evening air. She didn't seem to notice it. "I know we planned to go together, but that night we were supposed to leave, I realized I was in no shape to take care of you. I was so broken up by *Dat*'s death, and…and I was a mess. Do you remember how much of a mess I was?" When she said nothing, he continued. "I thought I knew what I wanted, but I didn't. Not exactly, at least. I wasn't mature like you. I'm only a year younger than you, but you know how it is with boys sometimes. You have one of your own." He gave a little laugh, hoping that might draw a smile from her, but it didn't.

He pressed on. "When I left, I planned to return for you. You have to believe me when I say that. Once I found a job and got settled, I was coming back for you. When I hitchhiked out of Faith's Run that night, I had a hundred and eight dollars, which wasn't nearly enough for one of us, let alone two."

"Did you find that man in Pennsylvania?" she asked quietly. "The one we heard would help Amish kids leave?"

"I did. I hitched and walked there. He and his wife were nice. I only stayed with them a few days before a friend of theirs drove me to a dairy farm in the middle of nowhere in Iowa. They were good Christians, the Hostetlers, and they were good to me. They had a bunkhouse for their farmhands. You couldn't have stayed with me even if we had married. Only single men were housed there, no girls were allowed. Not under any circumstances, not if you didn't want to get fired on the spot."

Lissie stopped on the grass path and put out her finger to touch a leaf where another monarch butterfly sat. "This time of year, they only live a few weeks. Remember learning that from your *dat*? They lay their eggs that hatch into the caterpillars and then die a short time later."

"Unless they're born late in the year," he added, standing beside her and staring at the black-and-orange butterfly. "Those fly south for the winter and come back here when it gets warm again. They live like…eight months. That always fascinated me."

She looked up at him, her dark brown eyes piercing. "Daisy's two months younger than Naomi."

Her statement surprised him. What did that have to do with the life cycle of a monarch butterfly? Nothing. That was just how Lissie's mind had always operated. They could be discussing one thing while she was thinking about something completely different simultaneously.

Thankfully, she didn't wait for him to respond.

"I heard them talking about their birthdays at the supper table," she said. "When I met Daisy the other night, I knew they were close to the same age, but I didn't realize they were that close." Her gaze never left his. "How did you meet her mother in the middle of nowhere, Iowa, Menno? Where is your wife now?"

He dropped his chin to his chest. Leave it to Lissie to dive into the hard stuff right from the start. "I met Heather at a truck stop on the interstate near the farm. It was where all the farmhands who stayed with the Hostetlers hung out when they weren't working. It was the only place to buy snacks. Three meals a day were provided on the farm, but…" He felt his shoulders sag as he forced himself to look at her. "But we were all young, eighteen, nineteen."

"All Amish?" she asked.

He shook his head. "Maybe half. Daisy's mother, Heather, waited tables at the truck stop." He was quiet for a minute. "I didn't plan it. But I was feeling so guilty about leaving you that I convinced myself I was a terrible person and you'd be better without me. Then it just…it kind of just happened with Heather."

She folded her arms and waited for him to go on.

Even though he'd practiced this part, Menno was surprised at how hard it was for him to continue. He couldn't read her face.

Given how many times he'd told his story, it should have been easier by now. He'd stood before an Amish church congregation in Iowa and confessed his sins. That was the only path to forgiveness. It had been the only way he was allowed to be baptized and rejoin the Amish church. He hadn't believed it could get any harder than that. He'd been mistaken.

He felt a burning sensation behind his eyelids, and he breathed deeply. He didn't want to tear up; that would only make things harder for both of them. He'd gotten this far; he would tell her the rest. He needed to, even if she never spoke to him again after hearing it.

"There was this guy who was picking on me in the bunkhouse. Playing practical jokes, saying mean things about my upbringing, saying crude things about me being friends with Heather." He wiped his hand across his mouth. "So Heather invited me to move in with her and rent her spare room. She said she needed the money."

Lissie raised an eyebrow. "You were bullied into moving in with a woman?"

He thought about that for a moment. "Not exactly. It was…more complicated than that. I was so lonely and missing you and…" He trailed into silence because he didn't know what else to say.

"So…" She urged him to go on.

"So…" He shrugged. "I moved in with Heather and she…got pregnant." He ran his thumbs behind the smooth leather of his suspenders. "I wanted to marry her as soon as I found out, but she said no. She said I was too nice a guy to marry a girl like her."

He saw Lissie's face soften, giving him the strength to continue.

"We had Daisy, and I thought we would be all right, but Heather didn't take to being a mother. I was the one who cared for our baby, got up at night with her and such. Heather went back to work at the truck stop. A neighbor in our trailer park watched Daisy while I was at work. Then, one night, when Daisy was three months old—" His voice caught in his throat and he hesitated momentarily. "One day, Heather told me she had to cover someone's midnight shift at the truck stop, and—" He met her gaze, his eyes growing moist. "She never came home to us again."

Chapter Seven

"*Ach*, Menno," Lissie breathed, her eyes welling with tears.

Studying him, she realized he was more handsome than she remembered. His golden hair shone from beneath his straw hat in the fading light, and she forced herself to look away. All evening, she had been trying to manage her unwelcome emotions. She didn't want to face her feelings for Menno. She didn't have the time or energy for the emotions that overwhelmed her, yet they were there nonetheless, thumping with each beat of her heart. Despite her anger with him, she could no longer deny that she still cared about him. The pain she heard in his voice hit her hard because, no matter how badly he had wounded her, she hated to see him in such agony.

"I'm sorry that happened to you," she whispered, shifting her gaze until she met his deep blue eyes. "And Daisy." One meal with his little girl and Lissie felt a tenderness she'd never experienced except with her own children. She was unsure why she'd had such an immediate response. Maybe it was because Daisy was motherless. She didn't want to feel this way toward his daughter either. It would only make it harder to leave Faith's Run.

"I tried to find Heather," he continued after a pause.

"I talked to people at the truck stop. No one knew anything, or at least wouldn't admit to it. But I didn't give up, and eventually I discovered she wasn't covering anyone's shift. She'd lied to me. That night, she did go to the truck stop but just picked up her paycheck, and left. The dishwasher told me he thought he saw her get into an eighteen-wheeler in the parking lot." He made a fist, brought his knuckles to his mouth, then lowered it. "I never saw her again. Never heard from her. Not a phone call, letter or birthday card for Daisy. I kept the same cell number, still have it, just in case, but…" He stared at his dusty boots. "She didn't want us. She made that clear."

"She left her *baby*," Lissie said softly, unable to imagine it. As bad as her marriage to Alvan had been, even the couple of times he got heavy-handed, she would never have abandoned her children to escape him. "I'm sorry," she repeated. "For you and Daisy both."

He began to walk and she fell in beside him. "I guess the good thing is that Heather left before Daisy was old enough to know she had a mother," he said. "For her, it's only been the two of us, so she doesn't know she's missing out."

"What did you do when you realized she wasn't coming back?" Lissie asked. What she really wanted to know was whether he had loved Heather, but she didn't dare put that question into words. And why did that matter to her? "Eunice said you returned to Faith's Run three years ago. Did you work on that farm in Iowa until you got here?"

He slid his hands into his pockets, keeping his eyes fixed on the path as they walked. "For a while, I tried to work on the Hostetler farm. I didn't know what else to do, and I kept hoping Heather might come back. The Hostetlers helped me when they could, giving me time off when I needed to take Daisy to the doctor and getting the things I needed for her. My neighbor kept an eye on her during the day while I worked, but by the time Heather had been gone a year, it was getting too hard to be a single father and a farmhand."

He paused for a moment, then continued. "And I missed our Amish community. Terribly. I missed *being* Amish, Lissie. I missed our gentler way of life, the support, our food." He chuckled. "I even missed the long, boring church services. I thought I wanted a pickup truck and a cowboy hat. I thought I wanted to be free from our *Ordnung* that controlled everything I said and did. But I'd been such a fool, thinking I wanted to be an Englisher."

She smiled nostalgically, remembering why she'd once believed she wanted to be English. She had dreamed of wearing blue jeans, going to a rock concert, and sporting a ponytail and dangly earrings. Those were foolish, materialistic dreams she had outgrown as she discovered more about herself. Now, at nearly thirty-one, she knew with all her heart that she was meant to be Amish.

"So what did you do?" she asked.

"Once I made up my mind that I wanted to be Amish again, I went to the local farmer's market. I picked an Amish man with a kind, fatherly face and told him my story. I asked a complete stranger for help." He pressed his lips together, seeming lost in the memory. "His name was Abe Yoder, and he told me his church would welcome me if I was willing to set myself right with *Gott*. That afternoon, after Abe closed up his bake shop, he took Daisy and me home with him."

"Just like that?" she asked. She shouldn't have been surprised. Menno hadn't been baptized. Even being a stranger with a child out of wedlock, it wouldn't have been too hard for him to return to the Amish faith because he hadn't officially joined the church. Their people went to great lengths to save their brethren.

"Just like that. Now, I won't say it was easy." He grinned wryly. "I missed some things about the English world. And I had bad habits to break. But the men and women in Abe's congregation helped me accept that I could be forgiven for my trespasses and that I had a place among them. We lived with Abe and his wife, Lettie, and they helped me take care of Daisy. I worked for Abe doing whatever he needed on his farm, embraced the church and community, and was happy there for a while. But I missed Delaware. I missed my family. So I moved back three years ago when Daisy was six."

"Your mother must have been so grateful to see you again," Lissie said tenderly. She knew it had to have been difficult for Elizabeth to believe she had lost her eldest son to the Englisher world. "I guess our congregation was pleased to welcome you back."

He tilted his head, first one way, then the other. "There was some grumbling, but Abe's bishop wrote a letter to Bishop Hamul, saying I'd reformed, and I was taken back into the fold."

They reached the pond, and she spotted her *dat*'s wooden rowboat tied to a willow tree. The boat looked to have been repaired recently and had a fresh coat of varnish. She turned to Menno, crossing her arms as a gentle breeze brought the scent of lilacs. "You returned to Faith's Run and opened the ice cream shop. Was that your plan?"

"I didn't have a plan. I just wanted to come home and raise Daisy near my family. I worked for my brother Jude for a while. He's increased *Dat*'s little dairy herd tenfold." He wrinkled his nose. "But I don't love cows."

Something about how he said it made Lissie want to laugh aloud, and she had to press her lips together to hold it in.

"But you know me. I *do* love ice cream. And no one sells homemade ice cream around here anymore." He opened his arms wide. "So *Grossmammi* and I started messing around in the kitchen with recipes and before I knew it, I was in the ice cream business. I started out selling at local places: Byler's Store, Spence's Bazaar and Fifer's Orchard. Business was so good that I could build a shop on *Mam*'s property."

Lissie didn't want to be, but she was impressed. How could she not be with everything Menno had achieved as a single father? And he was a good one, from what she could tell. Alvan had been an awful father, so it was hard not to be awestruck. But she was also overwhelmed by all that Menno had shared with her. It was difficult to accept the notion that he'd had a child out of wedlock; marriage was a cornerstone of the Amish way of life. Yet she had to reconcile that with the fact that he had not neglected his responsibility to Daisy. It would have been easy for him to leave her behind in Iowa, in the care of the Yoders. When he returned as the prodigal son, no one in Faith's Run would have ever known about his child born on the wrong side of the sheets.

They stood beside each other in silence as the sun dipped behind the trees to the west and the pond transformed into a canvas of fiery orange, reflected in the still water. Her father's rowboat bobbed gently, its silhouette a dark contrast to the cattails and reeds behind it. Tiny ripples disturbed the surface as fish, roused by the fading light, leaped for the last of the day's insects. Dragonflies, their wings catching the last glimmers of sunlight, darted across the water, and crickets and frogs serenaded the settling evening.

It was so beautiful that a lump rose in Lissie's throat. She hadn't fully realized how homesick she had been until now. It would be hard to leave again. "We should get back," she said suddenly. "The children will be wanting their ice cream."

"So that's it? You forgive me?" Menno asked.

She frowned. This was all too much for one day. "Of course I forgive you. The Bible tells us we must forgive others as the Lord forgives us."

He gave her a sideways glance. "You don't sound like you've forgiven me. You sound like you're still mad, Lissie. You look like you can't wait to get away from me."

She turned away and started back on the path to the house. "Your apology is accepted," she said stiffly. "That was all a long time ago. We were kids. We're adults now."

It only took him three long strides to catch up with her. "Don't you have questions? About Heather, at least?"

"There's nothing I need to know about her. She doesn't affect me or my children."

"Oll recht." He slid his hands into his pockets, sounding unconvinced. "Questions about your family farm? How I bought it? Why?"

"Menno, those things are your business," she said firmly. Sternness was an emotion she could handle right now—not the tenderness she had felt for him. "I have more important things to worry about than you. I need to find a job. I have to get the children settled and enrolled in school. I need to start a garden."

"Why do you want a job?"

"Because I have to feed my children," she snapped.

"My husband wasn't a man of means, and I won't take advantage of Eunice's generosity."

"*Okey.* I can give you a job."

She sped up. "The two of us working together wouldn't be a good idea."

"But I thought you forgave me."

His teasing tone pushed her past annoyance. Now she was angry. "That doesn't mean I want to work for you!"

He sighed with a mixture of what sounded like impatience and continued amusement. "Lissie, there aren't many jobs for Amish women around here. You'd probably have to go into town for a job. That's unrealistic for a widowed mother caring for her aging aunt."

"I'll figure it out, Menno. I don't need your help." They walked through a tall hedgerow blooming with pink and blue wild morning glories that divided one field from another. She was relieved to see the barnyard. She could get away from his handsome smile and playful voice if she could just get back to the house.

She saw him shake his head out of the corner of her eye. "So you don't want to work for me. Fine. I get it. Can you at least let me help you get your children to school and registered?"

"I can certainly walk them to school myself on Monday."

He nodded. "You certainly can, but it will be a bit of a hike. The Creek Crossroads school, where we went to, burned down earlier this year."

She halted beside the chicken house. "Oh no. Was anyone hurt?"

"*Nay.* A lightning strike in a storm. It burned to the ground, though. We're rebuilding once the planting is in, but the children around here are finishing the year at Rosedale. It's a long walk from here, and I don't like Daisy going so far on her pushscooter. I drive her back and forth, so I may as well take Naomi and Jonah. It wouldn't make sense for both of us—"

"Fine," she blurted, interrupting him.

"Fine what?"

She folded her arms tightly. "Fine, we'll work something out getting my *kinner* to school with Daisy. Fine, I'll go with you on Monday to register them with their teacher." She hated to agree to anything that meant spending more time with him, but she wouldn't sacrifice her children for her own comfort.

"Now you're coming to your senses," he said. "Will you think about the job, too? I've got a couple of positions I need to fill. You could work in the office. My bookkeeping is a mess, and you were always better with numbers than I was. Or you could scoop ice cream if you want. I also need someone to—"

"Nay!" She pointed at him. "I'm not working for you, Menno. So don't ask again."

He raised his hands, palms out to her. "Fine. I'm just saying I could use the help, and you—"

"Don't push me, Menno." She made a beeline for the house, thinking that moving to Tennessee sounded better by the minute.

Sunday was a visiting day rather than a church day, and as usual, Menno and Daisy found themselves at his mother's place by midafternoon. Elizabeth Bontrager's home was one of the busiest in Faith's Run on Sundays when their district and the nearby district didn't hold church, largely because his mother was such a wonderful host. She was also popular because so many of her patients appreciated her not only for her midwifery skills but also for her advice and lively conversation. With warmer weather upon them, there was always a spot under the shade of the silver maple trees for gossiping and a seat at a picnic table for what seemed like a never-ending meal. There was a volleyball net and a softball diamond for teenagers and single men and women, kickballs and hula hoops for children. There was also plenty of fence for the men to lean against while discussing crops and animal husbandry.

On their way over, Daisy insisted on stopping by Eunice's to see if she, Lissie and the children wanted to join them. He wasn't surprised when the older woman came out to the porch, frowning. She told him she'd tried all morning to get Lissie to agree to join her for visiting Sunday, even if only for an hour, but Lissie had been firm. Her niece insisted she and her children were too tired from their journey, and they all needed a quiet day to prepare for the week. Daisy had been sorely disappointed that Naomi wouldn't be accompanying them, but Eunice had cheered her up, promising that Lissie's children would be ready for school the following morning. Menno had invited Eunice to join him and Daisy—he'd even offered to hitch up his wagon, even though he preferred not to drive the wagon or buggy on Sundays when distance or weather required it. However, Eunice decided she'd better stick around so he and Daisy had gone alone.

Later in the afternoon, with a belly full of turkey and cheese sandwiches, pasta salad and lemon meringue pie, Menno wandered off from the laughter and chatter of folks gathered in the backyard. He needed a few minutes to himself to think. Unintentionally, he found himself behind the granary at the hog pen. He'd heard from

Daisy that the sow had given birth three days ago, but he hadn't had time to check the piglets out.

The sight of the mama sow and her little ones, no bigger than his hand, brought a smile to his face, lifting his spirits. He was disappointed that Lissie hadn't chosen to join them today, though he wasn't surprised. Their conversation the previous night had been intense. He didn't often discuss his past, seeing no need to rehash it all. He and Daisy were here now. He was a man at peace with *Gott*, focused on moving forward along his maker's path for him. It was clear their chat had been hard for Lissie as well. She had known nothing about Daisy or his life before his return to Faith's Run. It had all been a shock, which he hoped was why she had lashed out at him when he offered her a job.

The sound of footsteps behind him made him turn around. Menno watched his brother Jude, who was three years younger than him, approach. Jude was a redhead like their mother; Menno took after their dad. Jude was taller than him, slender, with their mother's blue eyes. They all had blue eyes, except for Junia, who had their father's brown eyes.

"Wondered where you got off to," Jude said. A toothpick in his mouth twitched as he spoke.

He was a serious man in both word and deed. Menno often teased him, saying he needed to have a little fun and laugh more. But that wasn't Jude's way. Jude was the serious, dependable one and for that, Menno was grateful. After their father died and their little sister was born, Jude took on the family farm's heavy responsibilities. For that reason, in Menno's eyes, his brother could do no wrong.

"Just checking out the new piglets." Menno lifted his

chin toward the sow lying in a patch of sun, nursing her little ones. "Eight?" he asked.

Jude leaned his lanky frame on the stockade fence beside him. "Nine. All healthy. Didn't lose a single one."

Menno nodded and they watched the piglets, listening to their delightful squeals as they tumbled over each other, trying to get to their mother's milk.

Jude cleared his throat. "Thought maybe Lissie would join us today."

Menno glanced at his brother. Jude hadn't just happened by and seen him here. He'd come in search of him. To talk about Lissie. "We invited her and her children. I think they're tired from their journey."

"Makes sense. Daisy said you had supper with them last night and that the two of you went for a walk."

"Daisy's a tattletale."

Jude smiled faintly. "That she is." He laced his hands together, resting them on the fence's top rail. "So you got to talk to Lissie. Settle things."

Menno eyed him. "I wouldn't say we *settled* things. She's still angry at me, Jude. *Really* angry. For something I did when I was nineteen years old."

"I can see that. Considering that loser she ended up marrying when you didn't."

"I didn't make her marry him," Menno defended. "And I was in no shape to be a husband to her."

Jude elbowed him. "I know. I'm just teasing you."

Menno watched a piglet climb over another and tumble comically off its mother's back. "You need to work on your teasing, *bruder*."

"So you say."

They fell into a comfortable silence.

"She's angry for sure," Menno said after a bit. "But I think there's still something there. You know, between us."

"Really? After all these years?"

Menno frowned. "Says a man who has never walked out with a woman in his life."

"I've walked out with plenty of girls," Jude insisted, sounding mildly offended.

"Maybe you've driven plenty home from a church supper or a singing, but you've never *dated* anyone."

Jude shrugged, plucking the toothpick from his mouth and sliding it into his pocket. "Haven't found the right one yet."

Menno thought about telling him that he needed to get a move on with that. At twenty-six, it was time he married. But that might lead Jude to point out that Menno was twenty-nine and still single, so he shouldn't talk. Instead, Menno went on with his thoughts.

"I feel like there's something still there," he said again, turning it over in his mind. "Like…like I still have a chance with her. *We* have a chance. She's still the woman I fell in love with when I was sixteen. She might not be that girl anymore, but Lissie is as confident, capable and beautiful as she was when we were together. More so."

"She still quick to anger? Argumentative?" Jude asked.

Menno smiled. "*Ya*, she is. But she was never a sweet, passive woman. That was one of the reasons I loved her so much."

Jude sighed. "You really think you have a chance with her?"

He thought before he answered. Did he truly feel a spark between them last night, or was that just wishful thinking? *Nay*, it was real. He looked at Jude. "I do. And even if I don't have a chance, I have to try. I'll never be able to forgive myself if I don't."

Jude met Menno's gaze and nodded. "Good for you." He clapped his brother on the shoulder. "I wish you the best. And I'll pray for you." He raised a reddish-brown eyebrow. "Because you'll need all the prayers you can get."

They laughed, and Menno's heart soared thinking that with Jude at his side, and *Gott* in the heavens, anything was possible.

Chapter Eight

As they approached the Bontrager family farm in Menno's wagon, Lissie tried not to pay attention to the white cement block building on the road front. Someone had painted a giant triple-scoop ice cream cone covered in rainbow sprinkles on the west wall. Looking at it, she could almost taste the mint chocolate chip ice cream. Earlier that morning, she'd seen the store when they passed it on their way to the one-room schoolhouse Naomi and Jonah would be attending. Her children had been captivated by the creamery on a country road in the middle of nowhere, and Daisy had proudly shared everything about her *dat*'s business. Jonah, who had never been to an ice cream shop, had asked if they could stop and get some. Thankfully, Eunice, who had joined them for the ride, explained that the store wasn't open in the mornings. She promised, instead, to treat him and his sister to a cone one day after school.

Lissie heard Menno flip on his signal to turn into his mother's lane and she glanced at him. "Why are we turning here?" she asked, assuming he was taking her and Eunice home.

It was generous of Menno to offer to drive them to school, but she wanted to go home. While she appreciated his kindness, she had already spent enough time with him for one day. The half hour she'd been alone with him on Saturday and the emotions she experienced were confusing. She didn't have time to think about her feelings for Menno Bontrager right now; in fact, she preferred to avoid them indefinitely. With her children in the capable hands of Jakob Fischer, their teacher and an old classmate of hers, she planned to start her job search today. She had no intention of visiting Menno's mother or anyone else.

"I'm getting my coffee and cinnamon bun, that's what we're doing here," Eunice explained. "Every Monday, I have coffee and a cinnamon bun with Sheba. I told you that." She paused. "Maybe I did. My memory isn't what it once was."

Lissie exhaled sharply. Somehow, she found herself sitting between Menno and her aunt after they left the schoolhouse, a situation Eunice had orchestrated. Sitting so close to him made her uncomfortable, mostly because his proximity stirred feelings she could barely remember. As he chatted and laughed with Eunice, Lissie had to remind herself that she and the man beside her were no longer teenagers with the freedom to explore attraction. They were now both parents with heavy responsibilities.

"Could you stop the wagon, Menno?" Lissie asked. "I'll walk home from here. I'll come back for you, Eunice. I mean to take the buggy later and see if Ann Yoder needs help at her quilt shop."

"Ann shut that down years ago," Eunice said matter-of-factly. "She sells her quilts to a fancy tourist shop in Lancaster now. She ships them there once a month."

"Then maybe she knows someone hiring," Lissie countered, refusing to be beaten so easily. She knew her aunt wanted her to take the job Menno had offered, but she wouldn't. "I can do anything I set my mind to. You know that."

"I told you no one's hiring." Eunice crossed her arms stubbornly. "No one except Menno. He hires more Amish women than anyone in the county."

"*Um*... I'm going to get off the road while you two figure this out," Menno said, his tone neutral. He eased the wagon off the pavement and onto the gravel driveway.

"Maybe the Yoders are hiring at the orchard?" Lissie asked hopefully.

Eunice chuckled. "Mae Yoder has three daughters-in-law working for her for free now. She's not hiring." She placed her hand on Lissie's knee. "Come up to the house and say hello to Elizabeth. She's eager to see you. And you can have one of Sheba's cinnamon rolls. Best I've ever eaten. If we were a few years younger, Sheba and I could put up a bake shop right next to Menno's. We'd outsell him for sure and certain."

Menno laughed. Today he wore a blue shirt that made his eyes look even bluer. Lissie kept catching the scent of his clean hair that smelled faintly of the peppermint castile soap he'd always used. It was distracting.

"I don't doubt that. My *grossmammi* makes some incredible cinnamon rolls." He glanced at Lissie as he pulled back on the reins, stopping the wagon. "Eunice is right. *Mam* would love to see you. She was disappointed that you and your *kinner* didn't join us yesterday. I can give you a ride home later."

Lissie stared straight ahead, ignoring how handsome he looked in his fresh shirt, straw hat and fancy Englisher sunglasses that read *Ray-Ban* on the side. "I've two legs perfectly capable of walking home."

"Of course you do. But I'll have to take Eunice home in

a bit, anyway. You could have a visit and I can take both of you home. Or I can run Eunice back later and you can walk whenever it suits you. *Mam* doesn't start her office hours until ten today."

"Come now," Eunice cajoled, plucking Lissie's dress sleeve. "You know you want to."

Lissie's conviction wavered. She did want to see Elizabeth and would love to try one of Sheba's pastries. She'd always had a sweet tooth, and there hadn't been many treats in Alvan's home or his parents'. There had been enough food to eat, but anything beyond bland nourishment was considered excess and, therefore, gluttony in their strict household.

Menno tilted his head toward hers until it nearly touched her starched white prayer *kapp*. "Just one cinnamon roll, still sticky and warm from the oven," he tempted softly. "And you'll be on your way."

Lissie intended to protest, but she astonished herself when she threw up her hands and said, "Fine. But I can't stay long. I have things to do."

Menno grinned but had enough sense not to say anything more. Five minutes later, he dropped them off at the house and she walked into his mother's kitchen.

"Lissie, there you are, at last. Goodness, but it's good to see you." Elizabeth Bontrager rushed across the room to pull her into a tight hug. "And I'm sorry for all your trials, but you're home now," she whispered in her ear. "You and your *kinner*."

Lissie was surprised by the emotion that washed over her as she returned Elizabeth's embrace. Hugs from adults had been a rarity for her since she left Delaware. She'd always liked Elizabeth and admired her willingness to express her feelings, good and bad. It was something her own mother had been unable to do. "It's good to be home."

"And a bit overwhelming, too, I imagine." Elizabeth leaned back, looking into Lissie's eyes. "Give yourself grace, *ya*? Change is never easy, even when you seek it."

Lissie smiled at Menno's mother. She was her height with bright red hair, brown eyes, a freckled complexion and a smile that lit up a room. Except for a few tiny lines at the corners of her eyes, she didn't look like she'd aged a day in the decade since Lissie last saw her.

"We've come for coffee and cinnamon rolls," Eunice announced, taking mugs from a cabinet. She inhaled deeply. "I smell the cinnamon. Where's Sheba hidden them?"

"Where my grandchildren won't find them," Sheba said, coming out of the walk-in pantry with a plate of pastries in her hands. "The rascals ate the first dozen I baked before breakfast."

The three women refused Lissie's help, and she found herself seated at the plank oak table in the middle of the large kitchen that easily sat ten. There was a pot of tea for Eunice and Sheba and mugs of strong coffee for Lissie and Elizabeth.

"Tell me how you are," Elizabeth said as she put a cinnamon roll the size of her fist on Lissie's plate. "I can't imagine how hard the decision to leave Ohio was."

"Not that hard," Eunice said as she placed two rolls on the plate in front of her. "They didn't have their own house when her husband passed. Living with the in-laws, weren't you, dear?"

Lissie cut her eyes at her aunt.

"Hush, Eunice," Sheba chastised. "And pass me the buns. I haven't had but one yet, and they're nearly gone."

Lissie reached for her coffee, and Elizabeth slid a small stoneware pitcher of cream and a bowl of sugar toward her. "Oh, I just drink it black," Lissie said.

"Not anymore, you don't. You need a little meat on your bones." Elizabeth raised her chin in the direction of her mother and Eunice. "Now you two behave yourselves, or Lissie and I will take our coffee to the parlor."

"Who's not behaving?" Sheba argued, then took a big bite. "Mmm, that's *goot* if I don't say so myself."

"But you did say," Eunice reminded. "Don't let the bishop hear you bragging or you'll be faulted for *hockmut*."

"I'm not being boastful." Sheba blinked behind her eyeglasses. "The Bible says nothing against honesty."

Elizabeth eyed the two older women sternly and returned her attention to Lissie. "Eunice told me a little about your husband's death. I'm so sorry. Only a woman who's lost a husband can know the pain of another wife's loss. And even then, we can't really because each of us is as different as *Gott* created us to be."

"Thank you," Lissie murmured. She sliced off a piece of the treat in front of her using her coffee spoon. Closing her eyes briefly, she inhaled the warm aroma of cinnamon, the buttery richness of the dough and the vanilla cream cheese frosting. Then she took a bite. "Oh," she exclaimed, overwhelmed by its deliciousness. "Sheba, this is so—" She grabbed a cloth napkin and pressed it to her mouth. "It's been so long since I've had—" Tears suddenly welled in her eyes, and she stared at the plate, embarrassed. How long *had* it been since she'd enjoyed a sweet treat made with love?

When she looked up, Elizabeth was watching her. "Lissie, tell me what you need," she said. "How can I help make all these changes you're going through easier? What can I do for your children?" She eyed the shabby dress Lissie wore. "For you?"

Feeling self-conscious, Lissie poured cream into her coffee. She added a lot, just like she used to before marrying Alvan. "N-nothing. We don't need anything." She forced a smile as she stirred a generous spoonful of sugar into the mug. "We have everything we need. Eunice has been more than generous."

"She thinks she needs a job." Eunice slurped her coffee. "I told her we'd make out just fine without her going off and getting a job first thing. But she won't listen to me."

"Menno offered her a job," Sheba added. "But she won't have it."

Lissie glanced across the table at Menno's grandmother. "How did you know—" She halted midsentence. There was no need to ask how Sheba knew. Menno had told her. He and his maternal grandmother had always been close. The whole Bontrager family was like that. They told each other everything.

"You want a job?" Elizabeth asked.

"I need my own money," Lissie said. In case she decided to go to Tennessee. *In case this is all too much*, she thought.

Elizabeth sat back in the oak ladder chair. "Of course you do. We all need a little pin money." She glanced at Sheba and Eunice, concentrating on their pastries, then back at Lissie. "My *sohn* offered to hire you?"

She nodded. "But I…" Lissie made herself meet Elizabeth's gaze. "I don't think that would be wise. For either of us," she added after a hesitation.

Elizabeth studied her a moment longer, eyebrows raised, then took up her coffee. "I agree."

"I told her there aren't any jobs to be had for a woman around here," Eunice said. "Not with the hours she needs to keep with her *kinner*. Especially with school soon to be let out for the summer. And she's talking about putting a garden in." She harrumphed. "All too much, if you ask me."

Elizabeth crossed her arms. "I understand why you wouldn't want to work for Menno, but I have a thought. Would you be willing to work for me?"

Lissie had picked up her spoon, but set it down loudly on the plate. "For you?"

"*Ya*, I could use someone with some maturity and good sense. The billing, scheduling and recordkeeping, it's too much for me to handle on my own anymore. I have more patients than ever, and it's not as if I'm getting younger. I have a couple of employees who come and go, but usually the minute I get them trained, they marry, quit, and soon they're coming to see me expecting themselves."

Lissie didn't know what to say. A job so close to home that didn't involve Menno sounded perfect. "I… I've never done any of those things."

"Even better. No bad habits for me to break. You're a smart woman and a hard worker. I can teach you." Elizabeth lifted her cinnamon roll. "I don't need you every day. A flexible schedule would work best for me, if that suits you. We decide week to week, but your children are welcome here anytime. Daisy comes with her with *dat* when she isn't in school, and Junia would be thrilled to have another girl in the house. And another boy to boss around the way she does her brothers."

Lissie turned the generous proposal over in her mind

as she took another bite. Elizabeth was right—it would be convenient to work so close to home and bring Naomi and Jonah with her. She knew Eunice could keep an eye on them for her, but this was a better solution.

"You're sure you need help?" Lissie asked Elizabeth. "You're not just offering me—"

"This isn't charity. The question isn't *if* I need help, it's if you're interested in the job. I'm going to hire someone. Why not you?" Elizabeth dabbed her mouth with her napkin. "But I warn you, we have stressful days. Not all good outcomes. And as more folks move to Faith's Run, I have more first-time mothers. But you already know what it's like with that first baby, especially if you aren't living close to family."

Lissie nodded, remembering how scary it had been carrying Naomi and being so far from family and friends. "Could I think on it?" she asked Elizabeth.

"You can, but I plan to put word out this week that I need help."

Lissie hesitated. She knew she probably ought to think longer on the offer, but if there were no jobs in town, it didn't make sense to give up this opportunity. Strike while the iron's hot, her mother used to say. "I think I would like to try it." Her words came out sounding braver than she felt. She'd never had a job before and knew nothing about how a medical office worked except for what she'd observed at medical appointments for herself and her children.

"Excellent. You want to start today?" Elizabeth downed the remainder of her coffee.

Lissie froze. "Today?"

Elizabeth glanced at the kitchen clock on the wall.

"Why not? I have time before appointments start. I can show you around the office and explain your responsibilities. With no patients until ten and no women laboring here right now, there shouldn't be too many interruptions." She pointed to Sheba and Eunice. "As long as these two can stay out of trouble."

Sheba and Eunice looked at each other and grinned. "I think we can keep ourselves busy," Sheba said. "Eunice said she'd help me with my chores."

"I don't remember saying that," Eunice complained good-naturedly.

"Why don't we try it for a week or two?" Elizabeth suggested to Lissie, ignoring the other two women. "And if it's not right for either of us, we'll find something else for you. That *isn't* working for Menno." Her blue eyes twinkled with amusement. *"Oll recht?"*

Lissie smiled back. She liked the idea of working in an office with expectant and new mothers. She'd had dreams of being blessed with many children. That hadn't come to pass, but maybe this would be a way for her to fulfill her need to care for others. "I'll do my best." She pressed her lips together, fearing she might tear up again. "Thank you, Elizabeth. Truly."

Menno's mother covered Lissie's hand on the table with hers. "Hold off on the thank-yous until you've seen the mess my records are in." She pulled the serving plate of cinnamon rolls toward them. "Now we'd best split this last one before those two get it."

Everyone laughed and Lissie felt her heart melt. It seemed wise not to stay in Faith Run with Menno, but she wasn't sure she could leave again because, for the first time in many years, she felt like she belonged somewhere again.

* * *

When Menno hadn't heard from Eunice by twelve thirty, he walked from the building where his employees made ice cream to the house, searching for her and his grandmother. He assumed Lissie had walked home after having coffee with his mother, but he didn't know where Eunice and Sheba could be. He searched the kitchen, the sewing room, and even the parlor where they sometimes hid to nap, but he didn't find them. Not seeing them in the house, he stood on the back porch, wondering where they could have gotten to. If he didn't take Eunice home soon, she'd have to stay until he picked up the children from school.

He had an appointment with an advertising company soon. Thankfully, his meeting was over the phone rather than in person. Due to their businesses, their bishop allowed him and his brother to have a landline in their shared office. There had been some complaints from certain elders about the risks of letting Englisher technology into their lives. Bishop Hamul, however, was a wise man who understood the necessity of sometimes bending the rules to maintain their community.

As Menno walked down the porch steps, he heard his grandmother's laughter but didn't see her. Following the faint sound of her and Eunice talking, he walked around the side of the house. "Sheba?" he called. She'd always preferred her grandchildren call her by her given name rather than *grossmammi* or some form of grandmother. She said being a grandmother didn't make her feel old, but being called one did. "Eunice?"

"Over here!" his grandmother called. She stepped out from behind a small gardening shed that had once served as an outhouse.

He strode across the grass toward them. "What are you doing out here?"

Sheba held up a pair of gardening shears. "Morning glories in my blackberry hedge. They'll choke them out if I don't cut 'em out soon."

Eunice came from behind the building, also holding gardening shears. Both women wore men's flat-brimmed straw hats and long-sleeved men's shirts that looked like they'd come out of the rag bag. He frowned. "Is that my hat?" He pointed at Eunice's head. Even though he lived down the road now, he still kept spare clothes and such at his mother's because he spent so much time there.

Eunice shrugged. "I don't know. Found it in the mudroom. It's hot out."

He sighed. "Fine. I don't need it right now."

"*Nay.* I can see that, not when you've got that nice white paper hat." Eunice pointed at him, grinning.

Menno reached up and felt the disposable hat he wore in the commercial kitchen when they made ice cream. All his employees wore them on ice cream–making days. He snatched it off his head. "I guess you don't want a ride home?" he asked her.

"*Nay.* In a while, Sheba will drive me to my place in her cute little courting buggy. I'll get my buggy, go for the children and pick up Lissie when I drop off Junia and Daisy."

He stared at the older woman. "When *you* pick up Lissie?" He shook his head. "Didn't Lissie go home?"

Eunice and Sheba looked at each other knowingly before his grandmother spoke. "She stayed."

Eunice grinned. "To work."

"To work?" he repeated.

"*Ya.* For Elizabeth."

Menno stood for a moment, processing what he thought he had just heard. When he concluded, partly from the expressions on the two women's faces, that he had not misunderstood, he turned abruptly. Striding toward the back of the house where his mother's office was located, he angrily crumpled the paper hat in his hand. "No, you did not hire her out from under me," he murmured under his breath, knowing full well that his mother had.

Chapter Nine

Checking to be sure Lissie was nowhere in sight, Menno slipped into his mother's waiting room. Once inside, he made a beeline for the back, keeping his head down to avoid eye contact with patients. Or Rose. He wasn't in the mood to be flirted with. Head lowered, he went past the reception desk and down the hall. Spotting his mother's office door slightly ajar, he ducked inside. She wasn't there, but he'd wait for her.

There were chairs in front of her desk, but Menno was too wound up to sit. He paced the small room, moving between the wall where his mother's nursing degree and qualification certificates hung and the wall featuring a large bookcase. It was unheard of for an Amish woman to have a college degree, but she'd grown up in Canada among a unique sect and had been encouraged to pursue a career in midwifery for the benefit of her community. Thankfully, when she married his father and joined him in Delaware, their bishop had the foresight to recognize what an asset she could be to their community and the entire Amish population of the state. Family, friends and neighbors begrudgingly accepted Elizabeth Bontrager's formal education, but the girls in Faith's Run still didn't attend school beyond the eighth or ninth grade. The Old

Order church districts in Faith's Run were progressive, but not *that* progressive.

Menno stopped in front of the bookcase filled with medical textbooks, stopping with his hands deep in his pockets. He turned sharply and walked in the opposite direction, wondering how long his mother would be.

He couldn't believe she had offered Lissie a job, knowing full well that he had planned to hire her so he could spend more time with her. His *mam*'s interference felt like a betrayal. She knew how happy he was to have Lissie back in Faith's Run and how hopeful he was to convince her to rekindle their relationship. He'd made it clear that he intended to marry her this time. So why would she do such a thing?

Menno heard a door open, followed by his mother's voice. "Good to see you, Trudy. I want you back in three weeks. Lissie's with a patient now, but she'll be out front soon. She'll set up an appointment."

The door closed and he listened to her footsteps. Her office door opened and she walked in.

Seeing him, she closed the door behind her. "Hmm, busy morning? It took longer for you to get here than I expected."

He was unamused. "You hired her to work for *you*?"

"Lower your voice. Otherwise, Elzy Shroder, who's sitting in the waiting room, will have her ear pressed to that door." She pointed emphatically at him. "And by tomorrow morning, everything we say will be common knowledge in the county, along with a few creative additions." She sat down at her desk.

He closed his eyes for a moment. It wasn't like him to speak that way to his mother, or anyone else, for that matter. He was just so…*frustrated* with her. He balled one hand into a fist and repeated his question, this time more softly. "You hired Lissie to work for you?"

"I did." She slid on her reading glasses, flipped open the medical record and studied it. She wasn't going to make this conversation easy for him.

"Why?"

She didn't lift her gaze. "She needs a job to take care of herself and her children. She doesn't want to be a burden to Eunice. Totally understandable."

"But I told you *I* was going to hire her."

She looked up. "And she told me she didn't want to work for you." She returned her attention to the record. "Which is reasonable, considering the circumstances."

He began to pace again but managed to keep his voice at an acceptable volume. "How is that *reasonable*?"

She exhaled impatiently, closed the folder and sat back in her chair. "Because you broke her heart when you left her without saying goodbye, *sohn*."

He threw up his hands. "I know! I know that. But I'm trying to fix that. Fix *us*."

When she didn't respond, he halted directly in front of her, meeting her gaze.

She shook her head slowly. "Given the past you two share, it will be an uphill climb with her. Lissie's a wounded woman, and not just because of what happened between you. She hasn't had a good life since leaving here." She picked up her pen and tapped it on the desk. "Are you absolutely sure this is what you want, *sohn*?"

"It's absolutely what I want. I love her. I've loved her since we were kids, and… And I love her more now than I did the day I left her. I'm a man now. I know who I am, and I know what I want. I want her. I want to take care of her and her children. I love her. And I think she still loves me, too," he added quickly. "She's just not ready to admit it. But she will. She'll be ready eventually, and I want to be right in front of her when she is."

She studied him until the silence grew uncomfortable. He often sensed what his mother was thinking before she spoke, but he couldn't now. He hoped she wasn't opposed to him marrying Lissie, because that would hurt him deeply. It wouldn't deter him from trying to rekindle the relationship, but it would hurt.

At last, his mother's features softened. "You really do love her, don't you?"

He pressed his hands to the top of her desk and leaned forward. "I do. And I don't know that I can live my life without her. I mean, I know I can. But I don't want to, *Mam*."

She sighed. "*Oll recht*. Then I'll support you. Because I want you to be happy. We all do, Menno. Your *grossmammi*, , your brothers, your sister."

"*Danki*," he said in an exhalation of relief. "I needed to hear that right now."

She raised a finger in warning. "I support you, but that doesn't mean I won't speak up if I think you're taking a misstep. Hiring her would have been a mistake." She patted the file in front of her. "It's better that she works for me. Because I need her more than you do. And this will keep Lissie around without you being her boss. Ordering Lissie around is not the way to her heart, I can promise you that."

He opened his mouth to argue that he wouldn't be ordering her to do anything, but thought better of it and remained silent.

"The other thing I'm going to suggest," she continued, "is that you relax." She motioned with her hand, pressing it down slowly. "Don't try to tackle everything with Lissie at once. I know you want to marry her, but she doesn't need to hear that right now. She doesn't need a beau. What she needs is a kind neighbor. A friend who asks nothing of her except to be her friend."

He saw her point, but he had wanted this for so long that he couldn't imagine not pursuing Lissie now that she was finally here. "I can see soundness in that. But I don't want her to think I'm not interested. How long will it take before other single men are at her doorstep?"

She rose from her chair, picking a stack of medical records from the corner of her desk. "I have patients to see." She walked to the door. "Why don't we talk more about this tonight at supper?"

"We are *not* discussing Lissie at supper. Sheba and my three brothers will all want to put in their two cents." He frowned. "Junia, too."

His mother smiled, her dark eyes twinkling mischievously as she went out the door. "I know. Won't it be fun?"

Lissie heard Menno's raised voice from the hall, and although she couldn't determine exactly what he was saying, she sensed that his anger had something to do with her because she heard her name spoken. Lissie's first impulse was to walk in and confront Menno, but she reconsidered. On her first day of work, it didn't seem right to cause a scene. Instead, she bit her tongue, walked past the closed office door and continued with the duties her new boss had assigned.

By day's end, she was glad she had because she discovered she loved the job. She liked everything about it, from scheduling and cleaning exam rooms to setting them up again and sitting with a nervous client. Because

Eunice and Sheba picked up the children from school, Lissie stayed at the office until four. With no clients or employees around, she finally brought up the topic of Menno as she and Elizabeth restocked the exam rooms for the next day.

"Elizabeth, I need to talk to you," Lissie said, folding a freshly laundered cotton dressing gown used by patients.

"*Ach*, please don't tell me you're quitting." She blew out a sigh. "You're the best woman I've ever had here. You have the right balance of knowing how to keep appointments running on time while giving our clients the attention they need. I heard you talking to Ina. Even though she proudly proclaimed she was carrying her tenth baby, you took the time to talk with her about her varicose veins."

Lissie pressed her lips together to stifle a smile. She wasn't one to dwell on compliments, fearing it would inflate her pride, but she couldn't help feeling good. In Alvan's household, there had been no compliments, no matter how hard she tried to meet his expectations.

"*Nay*, I don't want to quit. I love working here," Lissie said, unable to restrain her pleasure. But then she turned to her, sobering. "But if it's best I not work for you, Elizabeth, I'll understand."

"Not work for me?" She closed a drawer loudly. "Why would I not want you to work for me?"

Lissie hesitated. She didn't want to upset Elizabeth, but she wouldn't be the one to come between her and her son. She'd find another job in Faith's Run. If she couldn't, she'd write to her brother, explain the situation and ask for money for bus tickets to Tennessee. Perhaps that would be better in the long run. Maybe it was foolish of her to think she and Menno could ever live in the same town again.

Elizabeth studied Lissie's face for a moment and

then rolled her eyes. "Ach, you heard our conversation. Menno's and mine."

"*Nay*, I didn't hear what you were saying," Lissie explained quickly. "I wasn't eavesdropping. But I heard Menno raise his voice, and I—" She hugged the folded gown to her chest, looking down. "I assume he doesn't want me to work for you."

Elizabeth took the gown from Lissie and added it to a folded pile. "I'm sorry you had to hear that. My boys don't use good judgment when they get emotional. I always thought it was a positive thing, me teaching them to acknowledge their feelings and be able to express them." She widened her eyes. "But sometimes I wonder if that was a mistake."

Lissie couldn't resist a smile.

"It isn't that Menno didn't want you to work for me," Elizabeth said. "It's that he wanted you for himself."

"He and I already discussed that, and I told him no." Lissie frowned. "Why does he want me to work for him anyway?"

"Do you really not know?" Elizabeth put the stack of clean gowns in a drawer beneath the counter that ran the length of one wall.

Lissie crossed her arms. She supposed she had an idea but didn't want to say it out loud. What if she was wrong? Talk about prideful. Accusing a man of still being attracted to her after ten years without contact?

Elizabeth closed the drawer and faced her. "He still wants to marry you, Lissie."

So it was true. Lissie stared at the floor, turning that over in her mind. "But so much time has passed. So many things have happened to both of us," she said slowly. "I don't know how I feel about…him having feelings for me."

"I understand." Elizabeth hesitated. "Lissie, I'm just going to come out and ask you, is Daisy a problem for you?"

"Daisy?" Lissie drew back. Although she hadn't spent much time with Menno's daughter, she already adored her. She liked the idea of Daisy and Naomi becoming friends and thought Daisy would be a good influence on Naomi. Daisy was vibrant and happy, traits that Alvan had thwarted in his daughter. Theirs had not been a happy household, and Alvan had never paid attention to Naomi because she was a girl.

"I'm asking if it's an issue that Menno and Daisy's mother weren't married," Elizabeth said.

Lissie adjusted the scarf that covered her hair. Suddenly she was tired; it had been a long, emotional day. "That's not Daisy's fault," she said quietly.

The older woman smiled. "Of course it isn't. What I mean is, now that you know something of Menno's mistakes, poor judgment, or whatever you want to call it, do they affect how you feel about him? How you *could* feel about him?"

Lissie groaned. "I don't think my feelings about him have anything to do with Daisy. I believe in the forgiveness of sins. Menno has obviously made amends for his past and seems to be working hard to be the man he needs to be. But…"

"But?" Elizabeth pressed when Lissie didn't finish her sentence.

"But I was so angry with him for so long. I still am. I don't know if I could ever get past that," Lissie admitted.

"I understand how you feel, Lissie. I was angry for a long time after Menno left us. First, I lost my husband, then I had a baby, and then, my eldest abandoned me when

I needed him most. Menno hadn't died, but I knew there wasn't much chance he would ever return. I held on to that anger for some time, believing it made me strong and was what kept me going." Elizabeth tenderly brushed her fingertips across Lissie's cheek. "But eventually, I realized I was wrong. I saw that my anger was harming my relationship with the children I still had, my mother, my clients, and my community. I prayed to *Gott* to help me let my anger go. When I finally managed that, I began to heal."

Lissie heard truth in Elizabeth's words, but she wasn't ready to examine her own anger yet. Instead, she said, "I don't know what I'm supposed to do about Menno. About being home again. I'm confused. And overwhelmed."

"*Ach*, Lissie. That's completely understandable." The older woman wrapped her arms around her in a hug. "You've been through so much. The loss of the man you loved. The loss of a husband. And so much in between, things only you will ever truly know."

Tears welled in Lissie's eyes. "What if I don't belong here anymore, Elizabeth? What if my children don't belong here?"

"You *do* belong in Faith's Run. As do your *kinner*." Menno's mother gave her another squeeze before she stepped back. She offered a handkerchief from a pocket of her lab coat. "I think *Gott* brought you back to us for a reason."

Lissie dabbed her eyes. She wanted to believe that was true, but she had been wrong so many times before. After Menno had left the community, she'd convinced herself that *Gott* wanted her to marry Alvan. Then she'd thought He wanted her to stay with him, even when she realized he was not the godly man he had led her to believe. She had been wrong about so many things in her life. How could she trust any decisions she made?

Lissie looked at Elizabeth again. "What should I do?" she asked. "About Menno." She brought her hands to her cheeks. "I'm sorry. That was unfair to ask. He's your son." She lowered her hands. "You don't have to answer that."

"What do I think you should do?" The older woman studied her carefully. "Here's my advice as a woman, not as the mother of a man who loves you."

Lissie took in a sharp breath. Suspecting something was very different than hearing it aloud. *He still loved her... Menno loved her.*

"You do nothing for now," Elizabeth continued, guiding Lissie out of the exam room. "You care for your children, you pray for guidance, work here and become a part of this community again."

"But I see Menno every day," Lissie groaned. "We're neighbors."

Elizabeth walked down the hall, checking to be sure the lights were out in each room. "So treat him like a neighbor. As a member of your church. Maybe you become friends with your neighbor." She shrugged. "And if that's the end of it, then that's the end." She halted. "Everyone needs friends, Lissie."

"Everyone does need friends," Lissie agreed thoughtfully.

Elizabeth dropped her hands to her hips. "I should see if my *mam* needs help getting supper on the table. And you should get home. Naomi and Jonah will be eager to tell you about their first day at their new school. Do you want me to run you home in *Mudder*'s two-seater?"

"Nay." Lissie removed the heavy white apron she'd

been given to cover her clothing during the workday. "I could use the walk."

"Let me have that." Elizabeth reached for the apron. "I can take it home to clean."

"*Nay*, the linens I use here in the office are washed separately. You know where the fresh ones are. Just grab one tomorrow." She met Lissie's gaze. "You will come tomorrow, won't you?"

Lissie smiled. "Of course I will. And I'll take your advice. Menno's my neighbor." She nodded decisively. "I can be neighborly and nothing more." Elizabeth turned off the lights in the waiting room, and they went their separate ways, she to her kitchen and Lissie to her children with a new plan.

Chapter Ten

Lissie's plan worked well for weeks with surprisingly no pushback from Menno. She set aside any thoughts about their previous relationship and treated him like a new neighbor. She engaged in small talk with him on her front porch and at his mother's house, and they took turns driving their children to and from school. Some days, Menno would come by with homemade ice cream after work, and they would share it at a picnic table beside his dawdi house. Other days, at Eunice's insistence, he and Daisy joined them for supper. Lissie found that life became more comfortable when she separated the Menno of her past from the man living next door. She stopped dwelling on what had happened years ago and how the men in her life had harmed her and instead focused on forgiveness. She settled into her job, which she continued to enjoy, and the children adjusted to their new school and stress-free life. Naomi and Jonah began to blossom like the fruit trees in the orchard with no adult shouting orders, criticizing and limiting conversation.

On a Saturday morning in late May, Lissie decided to tackle a project she'd been putting off. The pantry was in desperate need of a thorough cleaning. When she had asked her aunt when it had last been scrubbed, Eunice had no recollection, joking that it had probably been whenever Lissie last cleaned it. With the kitchen windows wide open and the scent of the last of the lilacs in the air, Lissie moved everything from the pantry into the kitchen. Then, after sweeping out the linoleum-tiled room, she carried in buckets of water and a pile of rags.

Using a stepladder, she started on the top shelves. As she wiped, she listened to Naomi and Daisy chattering on the porch. Occasionally, there was a whoop from Jonah, followed by one of the girls reprimanding him. She supposed she should check on her son and see what he was up to. However, Lissie was hesitant to leave the pantry because she was enjoying her time alone. If her son got into too much mischief, his sister and Daisy would put an end to it or tattle on him.

It was nice for Lissie to have some time to herself. While her first weeks in Faith's Run had been good, they had been so busy that Lissie hadn't had much chance to think and process her past. Once supper was over and the evening's final chores were finished, she was tired and ready to go to bed as soon as her children were tucked in. On some nights, she was in bed before her elderly aunt, which amused them both.

Lissie smiled, thinking of her and Eunice carrying their lanterns down the dark hallway and giggling like girls. There had been a lot of merriment in the last weeks with her children, Eunice and their neighbors. It felt good to be a part of a thriving community again, and she didn't miss being under the thumb of Alvan or her in-laws.

The back screen door swung open with a bang as Lissie descended the ladder to rinse off her wash rag. As she dipped it in the clean water, she heard the patter of footsteps. "I'm in the pantry," she called to the children.

"Can we have lemonade?" Naomi asked.

"If there's any left!" As she wrung out the rag, Lissie studied the walls of the six-by-eight room with wall-to-ceiling shelves and a counter running down one side. The entire room needed painting, and she wondered how long it would take her. Did she dare start the project today?

"Knock, knock," a familiar male voice called. Again, Lissie heard the screen door in the mudroom open and close, followed by footsteps. These were heavier than the children's.

It was Menno.

Lissie felt a flutter in her stomach at the sound of his voice. As much as she hated to admit it, she was always happy to see him.

"Here you are," he said to the children. "I wondered where you'd gotten to."

"We were thirsty," Daisy said.

"*Mam* said we could have lemonade," Naomi explained.

"Lemonade," Jonah echoed. He followed his statement with a loud burp.

Everyone laughed, including Menno, and Lissie couldn't help but smile as she lingered, out of sight. Despite her efforts to resist Menno, there was no denying his charm. He was everything she remembered from their courting days: kind, thoughtful and hardworking. But now she saw more in him. From the perspective of a thirty-year-old woman, she appreciated the attributes that came with maturity: his devotion to their faith, his work ethic and his understanding of life's complexities. One of his most admirable traits was his closeness to his family and seemingly limitless dedication to his daughter.

"Any of you rascals interested in helping me fix a

fence?" Menno asked the children. "I figured out where Eunice's goats are getting out of the east pasture."

"Me! I wanna go!" Jonah jumped in. "I can help. *Mam* says I'm a good helper."

"I'll go," Daisy said. "I want to see the birdhouses. Papa and me built new birdhouses this winter."

"Can I go?" Naomi asked tentatively.

The hesitation in her daughter's voice made Lissie's heart ache. But she found solace in the fact that Naomi spoke up was an improvement. Before they moved to Delaware, she would never have asked to go with her brother. Alvan had been very clear about the duties of males and females and never included Naomi in anything he did. Menno was the complete opposite. He and Daisy cleaned stalls, fed their horses and made breakfast together.

"Of course you can come with us, Naomi," Menno said. "Where's your mother?"

"Hey, they can't go," Jonah protested. "They're girls."

Feeling guilty for eavesdropping, Lissie walked into the kitchen.

When Menno saw her, his face lit up. Square-jawed with chiseled cheekbones, he was even more handsome than he had been as a teenager. He had grown taller, and his shoulders had broadened. But his eyes were still the same bright blue, appearing even bluer framed by wisps of blond hair beneath his straw hat. "Hey," he greeted.

For a moment, Lissie felt as if she were tumbling backward to a time when she was a teenager, a time when life seemed so easy and simple. As their gazes met, she experienced lightheadedness, as if she had actually taken a tumble. The sensation was familiar, yet she couldn't pinpoint what it was.

"Hey," she returned, pressing her lips together so she wouldn't keep grinning foolishly at him.

He hooked his thumb over his shoulder. "We're going to fix a fence. The east pasture. I found Helen in my hostas again." He waggled his finger at Lissie. "But I figured out where she was getting through."

Helen was one of Eunice's elderly nanny goats. None of the herd of six still produced babies or milk anymore, but her aunt refused to get rid of them.

"They can't go," Jonah protested, wiping his mouth with the back of his hand. "They're girls! Girls don't fix fences. Boys do."

"We can go too," Daisy argued, planting herself in front of Jonah, her hands on her hips. "Naomi wants to go and she's my friend so we're going!"

"It's *oll recht*," Naomi said quietly, taking the empty glass from her brother and carrying it to the sink. "We don't have to."

Daisy whipped around to face her father. "Tell him, *Dat*. We can go, can't we? Girls can fix fences."

"Girls absolutely can fix fences," Menno said. He eyed Lissie. "Wanna go with us? It's a beautiful day. I'll let you hold the pliers," he teased. "Even if you are a girl."

Lissie laughed. "I've work to do. I'm cleaning the pantry."

He scowled. "It's too nice to be cooped up inside cleaning. And we want you to come." He turned to the children. "Don't we?"

"*Ya!* We do!" Daisy said, bouncing on her dirty bare feet.

"Would you come, *Mam*?" Naomi asked wistfully.

"It'll be fun," Menno cajoled. "Come on, Lissie. We're going to check out the new purple martin birdhouses in the meadow. We think they're starting to nest. They migrated all the way from South America. It would be rude not to say hello, at least."

Lissie dragged her gaze from him to Naomi.

"Please, *Mammi*?" her daughter begged, clasping her hands.

"I was thinking about painting the pantry," Lissie said, fighting the urge to go with them, but losing. Watching Menno with his daughter, she'd realized she kept her children fed and cleaned and instructed them in the ways of *Gott*, but she never had fun with them, not just for the sake of having fun. Not like Menno did with Daisy. Like he did with her children now. "It sorely needs it," she finished, not sounding all that committed to the task.

He shrugged. "Let's save that for a rainy day. I'll help you. *Gott* has given us sunshine, a warm breeze and purple martins to enjoy. Come on, Lissie." He tilted his head gently in the direction of the back door. "Come with us."

Lissie knew she shouldn't go. She had torn apart the pantry and had chicken to prepare for supper, plus laundry in the washing machine, but the expressions on Naomi's and Daisy's faces were pleading. Who was she kidding? She wanted to go because Menno had asked her.

"Oh, why not?" she said, throwing up her hands.

"Yay!" Daisy and Naomi squealed. Then they clasped hands and ran for the door.

"Come on, Jonah," Naomi encouraged.

"Fine," he grumbled.

For a moment, Lissie stood there looking at Menno, and he looked at her. She felt self-conscious under his gaze. She wore the shabby dress she had put on the day of her arrival, barefoot, with her hair knotted haphazardly beneath an old scarf. While he wore work clothes, there were no holes in his gray broadfall pants. His suspenders were not new but well cared for, and the leather was polished. His grass-green short-sleeve shirt was new, and she suspected his grandmother had made it. Despite her age, Sheba was an excellent seamstress. Lissie had commissioned her to make two dresses for herself and two for Naomi. She couldn't remember the last time they had new dresses; theirs were always hand-me-downs.

Menno spoke first, which was good because she felt strangely tongue-tied.

"This is good for your *kinner*, Lissie," he said quietly. "It will help them heal. And you, too."

She was afraid to contemplate what he meant by that. What did he know about her life with Alvan? She had a feeling it was much more than she had revealed to him, and she suspected who had been sharing information with him. She often saw him and Eunice in the yard, heads close together, speaking privately.

"I'll just take a short walk," Lissie warned. "Then I have to get back to my chores. And I'm not holding your pliers for you."

He laughed. "Fair enough."

From the back porch, Menno picked up a canvas tool bag and a small roll of heavy-gauge fencing, but Jonah insisted on carrying the tools. Daisy took the wire, agreeing to take turns carrying it with Naomi.

Together, they cut between the chicken coop and the barn, taking the path toward the pond and opting for the longer route instead of cutting through the pastures. Halfway to the pond, the path split, and they veered toward the meadow. The children raced ahead, chattering about the upcoming end-of-year school fundraiser and family picnic. Naomi and Jonah were very excited, as they had never attended a family event at school. In Ohio, their school attendance was inconsistent, depending on how often they moved, and Lissie often home-schooled them. When they attended an Amish school, Alvan refused to participate in any community activities and wouldn't permit any of them to go.

"*Mam* tells you're settling in nicely at the office," Menno said, as he watched their children take off.

"*Ya*, I am," she said, feeling self-conscious. Since she began working for Elizabeth, she and Menno hadn't spent time alone. The children, Eunice or his family were always around so Lissie never had to worry about making conversation. "I like the job."

"*Mam* says you have a knack for it—doing three things at the same time and making it look easy. She likes how you are with her clients. She says you're a good addition to her practice and everyone who comes through her door likes you."

Elizabeth had said the same thing to her, but Lissie's cheeks grew warm. She glanced at him, squinting in the bright sunlight. His sunglasses had rested on the flat brim of his straw hat when he'd entered the house, but now he was wearing them. She couldn't see his eyes, which was a good thing. For years after her marriage to Alvan, she had seen Menno's blue eyes in her dreams and felt guilty about it. She had begged *Gott* to take away the images; in time, they had faded, but they had never left her memory.

"I like that things are never dull," Lissie said. "I enjoy talking with the clients and doing things like scheduling and accounting, too. I'm finding I have a knack for numbers."

"Doesn't surprise me." He slid his hands into his pockets and walked slowly, his gaze fixed on the dirt path worn down over the years. "You were always quick to learn." He chuckled. "Quicker than me when we were in school, for certain."

"That was only because you spent your time figuring out how to get out of schoolwork while I was *doing* it."

"Don't do that," he said quietly.

"Do what?" she asked. They walked side by side on the narrow path, so close that the skirt of her dress brushed his pant leg in the breeze.

"Minimize your worth."

She stopped, unsure whether she was flattered or annoyed. "Minimize? That's a fancy Englisher word."

"It means—"

She laughed, interrupting him. "I know what it *means*, Menno. I may never have lived with Englishers, so I don't know some of their fancy words, but I used to be a reader, remember? I'd get books at Spence's Bazaar every week."

"And read them so fast that the bookshop lady would let you trade them in the next Friday." He laughed. "I remember."

Lissie covered her mouth to hide her grin. "*Dat* was so concerned that he went to the bishop, asking if I should be allowed to read at my age. He wondered if I should have been spending more time preparing for my duties as a wife and mother."

"I'm serious about what I said, Lissie," he said, sounding thoughtful. "I know it's not an Amish thing—to throw compliments around—but not all praise leads to *hockmut*. Hearing something positive once in a while isn't going to make anyone overly proud. That's one of the good things I learned when I was with the Englishers."

Lissie didn't know what to say. She was curious about his life with the English, but this didn't seem like the right time to ask. Instead, she replied, "Thank you for the compliment, then. I like the job so much that it doesn't feel like work."

"I'm glad you do, but I have to admit, I would rather you were working for me."

It was on the tip of her tongue to tell him that she'd overheard part of his conversation with his mother, so she was well aware that he hadn't wanted her in the midwifery office. Thankfully, Naomi interrupted them.

"Mam!"

Lissie looked to see her girl standing at the hedgerow at the end of the path, clutching the roll of wire. "Is it *okey* if we go over?" her daughter fretted. "I told Jonah to wait for you but he wouldn't listen to me."

Daisy was already climbing the old-fashioned wooden ladder called a stile. It was A-frame in shape, with steps that went up and over an obstacle. When Lissie was a child, the hedgerow had been a four-foot-high wire fence, but it was now six or seven feet tall and overgrown with a tangle of poison ivy, thorns and wild roses. Jonah was right on Daisy's heels, lugging the tool bag.

"It's fine," Lissie called. "Just be careful. You don't want to fall into the hedgerow. It's full of briars."

"And stay away from the birdhouses!" Menno warned.

By the time Lissie and Menno reached the stile, their *kinner* had gone up and over and disappeared on the other side. "Want me to go first and give you a hand?" he asked as they stood side by side looking at the stile.

She snorted playfully. "Menno Bontrager! How many stiles did we climb together over the years?" Shaking her head, she grabbed the hem of her dress so she wouldn't get caught up in it and placed her bare foot on the first moss-covered wood rung.

He chuckled. "Too many to count."

"Then you know I can get myself over one," she said, scrambling upward.

"I know. I just wanted an excuse to hold your hand."

Near the top, Lissie grabbed the handrails and froze. She didn't know how to respond to such blatant flirtation. Should she chastise him? That was her first impulse, but she wasn't offended if she was honest with herself. His words made her feel good. When they were teenagers, before she and Menno officially began dating, boys always asked her to ride home with them from singings or to go for ice cream. People used to tell her she was pretty. Menno would say things like that. But that had been a long time ago. It had been a decade, two babies, and many tears since she felt attractive, and even though she knew it shouldn't matter to her, it did.

She took another step and landed on the platform above the hedgerow. From there, she gazed out over the bright green field of new clover dotted with white flowers. She was impressed that Menno kept it mowed just like her father had. It was mostly open, but there were a few trees and clusters of white and yellow wildflowers. In the distance, near the fence that needed repair, she spotted the new birdhouses the children had been telling her about that morning at breakfast.

Three sturdy, weathered posts emerged from ankle-deep grass, rising at least ten feet into the air. Atop each one sat a traditional purple martin birdhouse. Each house featured a tall peaked roof and multiple compartments, all whitewashed. Small round holes in what looked like windows and doors in each structure served as entry points for the martins. Now that the swallows had migrated to nest, Lissie knew that the glossy blue males and brown females would peer from the entrances and chirp from the rooftops of Menno's birdhouses all summer.

She spoke over her shoulder. "You shouldn't say such things, Menno."

"Not even if they're true?" He placed one booted foot on the platform because there wasn't room for him and Lissie. He was so close that she could feel the heat of his body and smell his peppermint castile soap.

"Especially if they're true," she whispered.

"What's that?" He leaned closer to her.

She chose not to repeat what she'd said; she hadn't meant to say it aloud. She changed the subject. "The birdhouses are beautiful. I guess you had to replace the ones my *dat* made?"

"*Ya*, they were so old they were falling apart. The renters didn't maintain them."

"They're so beautiful, Menno. They look like farmhouses."

"I was wondering when you'd notice."

"Notice?" She looked at him, then back at the birdhouses. "Oh!" she cried in surprise, now recognizing a similarity. "They look like our house!"

"To the best of my ability." He sounded pleased. "I remembered how much you used to enjoy the purple martins."

She laughed. "We used to sit in the grass and watch them zip through the air at dusk, gobbling up insects. What were we? Fourteen? Fifteen?"

"Something like that."

His voice was soft in her ear, sending a ripple of pleasure through her that was unnerving. She turned and hurried down the other side of the stile. At the bottom, she landed barefoot on the soft grass. Menno followed behind her.

Lissie headed for the fence, observing her son trudge after the two girls while carefully avoiding the hotel-style birdhouses. "Daisy's been a blessing," she remarked. "She's helping Naomi come out of her shell, and Jonah loves her."

"*Ya*, I can tell by how he's always teasing Daisy." He walked beside her. "This morning, she found three worms in her barn boots."

Lissie laughed and then covered her mouth. "I'm sorry. I shouldn't laugh. That was very naughty of him."

Menno laughed with her. "It *was* naughty of him. And funny. He even added dirt so the worms wouldn't die. Daisy made him put them back in the compost pile."

"Sounds like something you would have done." She glanced at him, and he flashed a smile that made her smile back. "Thanks for making me come. You were right, it's nice to get out and walk the property." She lifted her face to the heavens. "The sun feels good."

They walked past one of the purple martin houses, and he brushed his fingers against the pole as they went by. She mimicked his motion, feeling wistful. She meant what she had said. She was glad she had come with him on this little excursion. But she didn't know what to do with that. Elizabeth's suggestion to think of Menno as a neighbor had been a good idea, but as she touched the place he had just touched, she wished they had done it at the same time. She imagined how it would have felt to accidentally touch his hand. Then she thought about holding his hand. When they were courting, they'd held hands whenever they were alone. She missed that kind of physical contact. Alvan had never been the kind of man who held his wife's hand.

"*Dat*!" Daisy shouted.

The little girl caught her father's attention, but instead of answering her, Menno hesitated, looking at Lissie. Their eyes met and she suddenly felt short of breath. She wanted to say so many things to him, but mostly she wanted to take his hand right now.

Then Daisy called to him again, and he slowly turned from Lissie not seeming to want to tear his gaze away any more than she did.

Chapter Eleven

"Daddi!" Daisy hollered when he didn't answer her.

Menno dragged his gaze from Lissie's beautiful face to see his daughter nearing the stockade fence. "*Dochtur*!" he called back, feeling more impatient with her than he wanted to. He wanted five more minutes alone with Lissie, to not be a father, a son, or a brother. He wanted to be a man spending time alone for a little longer with the woman he loved.

But of course, when a man was a father, he was always a father. And he was well aware that the choices a man made in his past carried throughout the rest of his life. He had never regretted Daisy's birth, but that didn't mean being a single father was always easy.

"Is this where Helen got out?" Daisy shouted. Naomi stood beside her, still holding the roll of wire. Jonah had dropped his bag ten feet from the fence and was busy climbing it.

"Sometimes I wonder about this girl," he said only loud enough for Lissie to hear. She chuckled, which was the response he was hoping for. He liked making her laugh; he always had. He took a few more steps and halted at the tool bag in the grass, raising his voice again. "Does it look like a place a goat might get out?"

Both girls looked at the obvious break in the upper fence and then back at him. "*Ya*!" they yelled in unison.

"Then that's where we start." He looked at Lissie again.

He didn't want to patch the fence yet. He wanted to stand right here in the warm sunshine under the shadow of a birdhouse he'd built just for her because he knew she loved them. He wanted to talk to her. He wanted to be with her because she seemed to want to be with him for the first time since she arrived. As much as he hated to admit it, his mother's advice had been sound. Treating Lissie like his neighbor rather than the woman he loved had been wise. By taking a step back from her, she seemed to be taking a step toward him.

"I guess I actually have to fix the fence," he said.

"I guess you do. But come on." She picked up the tool bag and walked away. "I might hold the pliers for you if you ask nicely." She turned her head to look at him with a smile, a smile for him alone… He would fix a hundred fences to see it again.

That night, after Daisy had gone to bed, Menno went outside to sit on his porch. Hours later, he was still reflecting on how Lissie had smiled at him today. He still felt the warmth of her gaze and remembered how easy it had felt to be with Lissie today. He settled into one of the two white Adirondack-style rocking chairs, gazing across the barnyard toward the big house. A light glowed from a window in the corner bedroom upstairs. It was the bedroom where Lissie slept. Was it too much to hope she might be thinking of him, too?

The sound of wheels on the gravel driveway drew his attention as a dapple-gray driving horse came out of the darkness. There was only one in Faith's Run, so he knew who was visiting so late. He watched his brother Jude roll up to the hitching post in front of the porch and climb out of their grandmother's antique two-seater buggy. Completely open, with four large wheels and a single narrow bench seat upholstered in black leather, it was the vehicle he and Lissie had ridden in on Saturday nights after they had officially become a couple. The memory made Menno sad but, at the same time, hopeful. Maybe they would ride in it together again.

"Evening," Menno greeted, surprised to see his brother. The day before, Jude had mentioned that he was going to a singing in Rose Valley and would be taking a young woman named Gladys home afterward. It was traditional for girls to arrive at singles gatherings in groups with friends or family members. By prearrangement or not, they had the opportunity to allow a boy of their choosing to take them home.

Nine o'clock seemed early to return from an event designed to help unmarried men and women find husbands and wives. When Menno was dating Lissie, it wasn't unusual for him to roll into this barnyard after midnight. Even then, they sometimes talked on the porch swing for another hour.

"Evening," Jude said, dipping his chin in Menno's direction. He tied up his horse and grabbed a square woven basket from the floor of the buggy. Without a word, he sat down in the other rocker and reached into the basket he'd placed at his feet.

Menno flipped the switch on the battery-powered lantern on the wrought iron table between them and watched his brother produce two amber bottles. Jude handed him one.

Menno held the bottle in the glow of light so he could

read the label. "Root beer. Nice." He twisted the cap off and took a sip. "Even cold."

Jude opened his bottle and flipped the metal cap into the basket. "A bag of ice in a plastic bag inside a paper bag in the basket. It won't work in late summer, but it's as good as a cooler on a night like tonight." He took a long swig from the bottle.

Menno watched him. "I don't think you packed this for me. I mean, if you did, that was awful nice of you, *bruder*, but..." He took another sip, narrowing his gaze. "Weren't you taking a girl home from a singing tonight?"

Jude leaned back in the chair and gave a push with his boot to set it in motion. "Didn't work out."

Menno observed him rocking for a moment before starting his own. "I'm sorry to hear that. Sick? Family emergency?"

Jude scowled. "She went home with someone else."

Menno squinted in puzzlement. "But I thought you asked to take her home when you saw her at Byler's Store the other day. She was getting an Italian sub, and you were getting the same thing, and you got to talking. Wasn't she the one who invited you to the singing?"

"*Ya*. I told her I'd come if she'd let me drive her home. And I thought things were going fine when I first met up with her tonight, but then—" Jude groaned. "After we got a snack and sat down together, I... I got nervous. And you know me. When I get nervous, I... I talk cows."

"Oh no, Jude." Menno pressed his head to the back of the rocker, looking up. "You didn't go on about cows."

"Cows and all things dairy," Jude admitted sheepishly.

Menno gestured emphatically. "Jude, we talked about this." He felt bad for his brother. He should have had a wife and a couple of children at twenty-six. He wanted to marry and have a family; he just didn't seem able to find the right person. "I told you, girls don't want to hear about milk testing and foot-and-mouth disease."

"Mainly, I was explaining bovine respiratory disease to Gladys." Jude sounded miserable now. He placed his bottle on the table between them and took a family-size bag of potato chips from the basket.

"You packed snacks, too?" Menno asked, impressed that his brother had thought of it.

"In case we got hungry. I thought I could take her the long way back to her place." Jude ripped open the bag, took a handful of chips and passed the bag to his brother. "Gladys lives in Hickory Grove."

Menno took a chip from the bag and crunched on it. "And you say she went home with someone else?"

"After we'd been talking a while, after *I'd* been talking," he corrected, "she went to find some napkins. When she never came back, I went looking for her. Spotted her talking to Eli Yoder. You know, from Seven Poplars. His *dat* owns that new chair shop out on the highway."

"Ah, the Eli Yoder with the curly hair." Menno made a corkscrew motion with his finger.

"All the girls like him," Jude said morosely.

Menno wanted to suggest that maybe Eli with the curly hair didn't talk about BRD, and maybe that was why they liked him, but thought better of it. "So she just rode away with him?"

"Nay." Jude took the bag from Menno's hand. "She marched up to me on his arm and told me she changed her mind. That she was going to let Eli take her home." He shrugged. "I left."

They were quiet for a few minutes until Menno said sympathetically, "I'm sorry, *bruder*. But at least she was honest with you. A few weeks ago, didn't some girl sneak off without telling you, and you found out later she'd ridden home with someone else?"

"I don't want to talk about that." Jude crunched loudly on the chips. "*Mam* keeps threatening to find a wife for me." He looked at Menno. "I'm terrible at this. Maybe I should let her."

Menno chuckled. "It wouldn't be the first time a mother hired a matchmaker for her son."

"*Nay*, not a matchmaker. That would be embarrassing. Everyone in town would know." Jude grabbed his root beer. "Enough about me and my miserable self. How was your day? Did you see Lissie? She give you a piece of her mind?"

"As a matter of fact, she did not." Menno grinned. "She went for a walk with me and the children and helped me fix a fence."

Jude placed his boots flat on the poured slab of the porch floor and ceased rocking. "She went for a walk with you? Of her own accord?"

Menno couldn't stop smiling as he got that same warm feeling again. "She did."

"And?"

Menno gazed up at the farmhouse. Lissie's bedroom light was out now. "And I think we've reached a turning point. I've followed *Mam*'s advice and acted like Lissie and I are neighbors. Today, I think I moved into friend land."

Jude's forehead creased. "Friend land? What does that mean?"

Menno sighed. "You really don't know anything about women, do you? If you want a girl to fall in love with you, first you have to become friends with her. You talk to her about things she wants to talk about. You listen to what she has to say. You discuss your thoughts, your dreams."

"You make friends with her," Jude repeated, sounding unconvinced.

"Exactly!" Menno brushed the salt from his hand on his pants and picked up his soda bottle.

"And once you're friends, you ask her to marry you."

Menno nearly spit out his root beer. "*Nay*, you don't ask her to marry you. Not yet. You…spend time with her. You woo her."

"So you're going to woo Lissie, now?"

"Eventually, *ya*. I hope so." Menno eyed his brother. "But I'm going to have to tread lightly. You know, because of our past. And she's been through a lot." He hesitated, thinking about how he intended to move forward with her. "With Lissie, I think the best thing is for me to let her go at her own pace."

Jude touched the neck of his bottle to Menno's. "Sounds like a good plan."

"*Ya*," Menno said, thinking about standing on the stile with her earlier in the day, so close that he could have taken her in his arms. He'd wanted badly to hold her but had known it was too soon. Not yet. "Now I have to try to be patient," he sighed.

Which wasn't going to be easy.

"Sure glad the rain held off," Annie Fischer told Lissie, standing beside her at a folding table inside the schoolhouse. They were packing the dirty serving bowls and utensils they'd used for the end-of-academic-year potluck.

"*Ya*. I don't think the barbecue sales would have been nearly as big a success," Lissie agreed.

The teacher, Jakob, Annie's husband, had come up

with the brilliant idea of combining an end-of-the-year picnic with a school fundraiser. The fathers of the children attending the two-room schoolhouse had rented two huge smoker grills from Byler's Store and begun smoking pork loins and whole chickens at dawn. Then, from 2:00 p.m. until 5:00 p.m., they'd sold meals to the public in takeout containers. Lissie and Elizabeth had made fifteen gallons of coleslaw the night before to contribute, and other women had prepared gallons of potato salad. By six o'clock, they had sold every available bit of food and had to turn folks away.

After the sale ended, fresh salads were brought into the schoolhouse from coolers in buggies. A brief recognition program followed, then children and their families enjoyed a feast of barbecue and homemade sides at picnic tables and on blankets in the yard. It would soon be time to go home, but a family softball game was still in progress, and no one seemed eager to leave. Gatherings like today were the glue that held an Amish community like Faith's together. Such get-togethers also brought joy and laughter to their lives, and Lissie found herself thriving in her new home with her aunt, Elizabeth and the others in the Bontrager family supporting her.

As she thought of her boss, her mind drifted to Menno. It seemed these days that she dwelled on him far too often. As hard as she tried to resist his charms, she couldn't help herself; she liked him. Maybe even more now than she had during their courting days. He made her laugh and was good at conversation. He cared about what she thought and, on more than one occasion, had asked for her opinion on something regarding Daisy. He confessed that as his daughter grew older, he worried he wouldn't always know how to properly parent her. He expressed concern about her not having a mother, which touched Lissie's heart.

With the convenience of him living on the property, she and Menno constantly engaged in activities together. They went grocery shopping, walked to church and, more often than not, shared the evening meal. Lissie told herself she had invited Menno and Daisy to supper frequently because their daughters were inseparable. She justified setting him a place at the table because Eunice enjoyed having him and Daisy around. But deep down, Lissie understood she was using others as an excuse to see Menno at the day's end. She wanted him there. And on the nights he wasn't, she missed him. She missed discussing their day at work and seeing how his face brightened when he walked into the kitchen and saw her.

"This yours or mine?" Annie asked, holding up a woven breadbasket with crumbs still inside it.

"Not mine," Lissie said, hoping her new friend didn't notice she'd been lost in thought. She hadn't grown up with Annie as she had with Jakob, but they were quickly becoming friends, and she was excited about building that relationship.

Annie dropped the basket into a large canvas bag. "Jakob said the rain probably won't start until early morning, but then it's supposed to pour. That will be a terrible shame because we were supposed to go to my in-laws' for Visiting Sunday tomorrow. And now we won't." She cut her large brown eyes at Lissie comically. "I just don't know how I'll stand it, having to spend a quiet Sunday at home. I'll have to sit in my parlor with my feet up, doing crossword puzzles, instead of running around fetching for my mother-in-law."

Lissie smiled as she eyed Annie's enormous belly beneath her apron. One of Elizabeth's clients, Annie was expecting twins in two weeks. And she had four children already. Seeing expectant mothers her age was one of the hardest things about Lissie's job. She tried not to envy others, but working in a midwife's office reminded her how much she wanted more children. Only being blessed with two children in ten years had been one of the many disappointments in her marriage. Of course, she had reminded herself often when Alvan was still alive that *Gott* couldn't bless a couple with children if a man didn't fulfill his duty as a husband.

Lissie laughed at Annie's comment. "With you about to give her two more grandchildren, she'll surely be running and fetching for you."

The look Annie gave her made Lissie laugh out loud, then they both burst into laughter. Annie laughed so hard that tears came to her eyes and pulled out a handkerchief to blot her rosy cheeks. "I like you, Lissie. That Menno Bontrager better know what a catch you are."

"Menno?" Lissie blinked, alarmed that his name would come up.

"He's handsome, *oll recht*. But you're beautiful. You make a good couple. The other day, I told my Jakob that you and Menno belong together, like peanut butter and jelly."

Lissie had started wiping down a dish before adding it to her basket but stopped. "Annie, I don't know what you've heard, but Menno and I are not—we're, um, not—" She stumbled.

Annie pressed her hand to the small of her back, waiting for Lissie to finish what she was saying.

"We're not..." Lissie felt silly even saying it. "We're not walking out together." She didn't know if that was what a widow called it when she started seeing a man. The only widows and widowers she had known in Ohio didn't date. A widow and her potential husband weren't even seen together. One day, the bishop would announce a forthcoming marriage, and when next the congregation met for services, the couple had been married in the interim.

"You're keeping it private. I understand. Some of our neighbors might think the rules are different for a widow. But you don't think anyone sees it?" Annie lowered her chin, looking up at Lissie through her lashes. "There's plenty of talk. The two of you are practically joined at the hip."

"But we're not—"

"Shopping for groceries together at Byler's," Annie said coyly.

"Well, it's silly if both of us need to shop, to take two buggies into town," Lissie explained.

"Driving the children to school together?"

Lissie crossed her arms. "Not every day. Just some days."

"Someone saw you eating donuts together at Spence's Bazaar—"

"With the children," Lissie interrupted.

Annie grinned. "You think no one saw your heads together while everyone ate supper tonight? Seated side by side on the same blanket?"

"But he forgot his—" She didn't finish the sentence. Menno hadn't thought to bring something for him and Daisy to sit on while they ate supper in the yard. It only made sense that they'd share with Lissie, Eunice and the children because Lissie had brought two blankets. Yet she could see from the look on Annie's face that it didn't matter what she said; Annie would believe what she wanted.

“We’re not dating,” Lissie said quietly.

Annie looped her arm through Lissie’s playfully. “Then you should be.”

Lissie sighed. “It’s complicated, Annie. We have a…a past.”

“Jakob told me. But this is the present,” Annie responded firmly. “And you should *go for it*, as the Englishers say.” She took Lissie’s arm again. “Lissie, I can see that he makes you happy, and the look on his face when he spots you?” She smiled. “*Gott* gifts us second chances sometimes. Accept the gift.”

Chapter Twelve

Lissie was still reflecting on what Annie had said about Menno when she slipped out the back door of the schoolhouse to load their belongings into Eunice's buggy. The sun would soon set and the softball game had finally ended. Other families were also gathering their belongings to head home. Was there truth in her friend's words? Did she and Menno make a good couple?

Lissie could no longer deny her feelings for him and knew he wanted to pursue a relationship even though he hadn't said so directly. So why was she fighting it? Was it because he'd left her? If so, was she punishing him for that by refusing to admit she cared for him? Was it that she couldn't forgive him? Or was it something else?

Lissie heard her mother's voice in her head. *So what,* dochtur*? You'll cut off your nose to spite your face?* Lissie had been an obstinate child and would agree that it was a trait she still possessed. Was she making a mistake with Menno out of stubbornness? Was she refusing to consider whether she and Menno could find happiness together because she was still angry about what had happened when they were kids?

"Caught you!"

Startled, Lissie whipped around, pressing a hand to her

chest. It was Elzy Shroder, one of the women from Eunice and Sheba's quilting circle. Lissie had never known her well but remembered her as a gossip and quick to judge others while seeing only piety in herself. "Elzy. You caught me by surprise."

The tiny woman scrunched up her face, gazing at Lissie through smudged, wire-frame glasses that perched low on her bulbous nose. While most women in Faith's Run wore colored tab dresses, Elzy always dressed from head to toe in black. Elizabeth thought Elzy believed her choice made her more Plain than other women. Menno's mother didn't have a high opinion of Elzy, but the feeling was mutual. Elzy disapproved of Elizabeth working as a midwife and often remarked that her sons "needed to step up to their duty and marry."

"I wanted to catch you alone," Elzy said.

Lissie didn't like the sound of that. "How can I help you, Elzy?" She smiled hesitantly.

"You can listen to my words and heed them."

The older woman stepped closer into the shadow of the buggy. Lissie took a step back.

"I'm going to say what no one else is willing to say to you, including your aunt. I like Eunice well enough. She's skilled with a needle and thread, but she's falling short in her responsibility to guide you."

Lissie crossed her arms. "What's this about?" she asked carefully.

"Menno Bontrager." Elzy brought a crooked finger to Lissie's face. "Are you aware that he's an Englisher and—"

Lissie stiffened. "Menno is not an *Englisher*!"

"He's an Englisher pretending to be Amish," Elzy accused passionately. "And that child of his? She was born on the wrong side of the blanket. I'm sure no one told you *that*. The girl is illegitimate, and that makes her a sin! A God-fearing woman like yourself can have nothing to do with a man like him. Now, I know that being widowed, you're desperate to find a husband, but—"

"I—" Lissie didn't want to disrespect an elder, but she was so angry that she could barely speak. How dare Elzy call their sweet Daisy a sin! While the Amish believed that folks were born in sin, that was not the same as *being* a sin. "I am not desperate for a husband, Elzy!"

The woman looked her up and down and sniffed loudly. "You should be! You're not getting any younger. That pretty face won't last forever, and soon you won't have the same choices you do now. You might find yourself married to a man twenty years your elder with a house full of another woman's children. And you won't be happy then, I'll warrant that." Once more, Elzy brought her finger to Lissie's face, and Lissie had to fight the urge to push it away.

"Elzy," Lissie said carefully. "I mean this with the greatest respect, but I didn't ask for your advice. And if you *ever* speak harshly of my aunt, Elizabeth, Menno or Daisy again—"

Lissie was surprised when Elzy took a stumbling step back, her expression one of shock. *Had no one ever put this woman in her place before?*

"If I ever hear you speak unkindly about my family," Lissie went on, her voice remarkably calm, "you and I will be talking with the bishop."

"About *what*?" Elzy snapped.

Lissie tapped her chin thoughtfully. "Hmm, maybe that passage from Proverbs? How does it go? Something about guarding our tongue to protect our soul?"

Elzy opened her mouth to speak, then clamped it shut. She started to say something again and then, without another word, stomped off.

At the same moment, Menno came from the opposite direction, turning his head to watch Elzy storm past him. He looked at Lissie. "Everything *okey*?" he asked, obviously knowing it wasn't.

Now that Elzy was gone, Lissie was shaking all over. She couldn't believe she had spoken to Elzy like that. She had never told anyone off, not even Alvan or his parents, who had certainly given her good reason. But to hear the older woman speak that way about Daisy and Menno? It had been too much.

"Lissie?"

She looked up to see him watching her. "I'm fine." She waved a hand dismissively. "You know Elzy. Putting her nose where it doesn't belong."

He tilted his head, studying her. He didn't believe she was fine; she could see it in his expression. Before he could speak, however, Daisy, Naomi and Jonah came around the corner of the building, all talking at once. Eunice followed.

"There you are," Lissie's aunt declared, blowing a raspberry. "I'm ready to go home if you are. Past ready." She pressed her hand to her belly. "I think that third helping of Sheba's molasses oatmeal pie may be my undoing."

Menno looked at Eunice. "Would you be *okey* with taking the children home?" He glanced upward. "I know you don't like driving after dark, but the sun hasn't set yet. And there'll be other families going our way. There's safety in numbers."

Eunice looked from Menno to Lissie and back at Menno, seeming to read that something was going on between them. "We'll make out just fine." She turned to the children, who were already scrambling into the buggy. "Won't we?"

They responded in a chorus of affirmation.

"Lissie and I will be right behind you. I have to help fold up the last of the tables from the church wagon and then we'll be on our way," Menno said. He glanced at Lissie, silently seeking her approval.

Lissie knew she shouldn't agree to ride home alone with him. Annie said people were already talking about them. Wouldn't that add wood to the fire? But she *wanted* to, and when did she ever do what *she* wanted? Others had controlled her for a long time.

Lissie leaned into the buggy. Jonah had already climbed up front, calling dibs on the coveted seat. "Behave yourself, young man." She glanced into the back. "The same goes for you two," she warned the girls.

Fifteen minutes later, Lissie sat beside Menno in his wagon, waving goodbye to the last of their neighbors as they left the school. It felt strange to be alone with him this way. The children usually accompanied them on outings, and their innocent chatter had always provided a buffer between them. It was easier to ignore her growing feelings for him in the company of others.

They pulled onto the country road, and he spoke as he urged his horse into an easy trot. "Out with it. I know that look. Something Elzy said upset you. Tell me what happened."

She stared at her hands in her lap, pleased that Sheba had finished her new peach-colored dress in time for her to wear it to the school event. "No need for you to get involved. I took care of it. Elzy means well enough, she just—" Lissie exhaled heavily. "She'll mind her tongue around me from now on."

"I would never get involved unless you wanted me to. I'm asking because you're upset."

A lump rose in her throat. *Should she tell him?*

"Lissie, there's nothing you can't say to me," Menno urged. "You know that, *recht*? We've been friends since we were younger than our children."

"She warned me to stay away from you," she blurted. "Because of Daisy."

"Because of *Daisy*?" For a moment he looked confused, then he frowned. "Ah, Daisy." He stared ahead. "Because her mother and I weren't married."

Lissie didn't say anything.

He turned to her. "Does that matter to you?"

"The Bible says a son shall not bear the father's guilt. I believe the same for daughters," she answered.

"I know you don't hold my mistake against Daisy. My question is, do you hold it against *me*?"

Lissie thought a moment before answering. "You confessed your sin. You asked for *Gott*'s forgiveness. That means you've been forgiven."

"*Ya*, by *Gott*. But do *you* forgive me? And I don't just mean for having a baby with a woman I wasn't married to. I mean for what I did to you."

Lissie listened to the clip-clop of the horse's shod hooves and the creak of the wagon bed, accompanied by the background sounds of chirping insects and croaking frogs. They entered a tunnel of beech and tulip poplar trees, and Menno flipped on the wagon's battery-powered headlights and taillights.

"Menno, you hurt me so badly when you left," she whispered.

"I know." He looked at her. "And I'm sorry for that. I am *so* sorry. I made a mistake—*nay*, a bunch of mistakes—and hurt so many people, you most of all. But I truly am penitent." He covered her hand on the bench seat between them with his. "I need to tell you something I've wanted to say since you arrived."

She waited as he took a deep breath and then continued.

"I still love you, Lissie. I love you more than I did when we were teenagers, making plans to run away and marry. I don't want to run away anymore." He met her gaze, stroking the back of her hand with his fingertips. "But I still want to marry you. And I want you to want to marry me."

His words should have shocked her, but they didn't. She knew he still loved her, and if she was honest with herself, she loved him, too. But could she move beyond their past? Could she push beyond her own?

"Menno, you understand I'm not the girl I was, don't you?" Lissie searched his eyes as the wagon rolled out of the darkness and into the last light of the day. "You've told me about your past, but I haven't shared mine." She swallowed. "With Alvan."

"Then tell me, Lissie. Maybe that will help us move forward." He squeezed her hand and then let go.

Lissie didn't know that she wanted him to be privy to all that had transpired when she was Alvan's wife. But Menno was saying he loved her. Didn't he have a right to know everything about her? She turned that thought over in her mind. She wasn't sure whether she owed him. She wanted to tell him, but she was afraid.

"We're almost home. The children," she said, her voice shaky.

"They'll be fine with Eunice. We'll go the long way home and you can tell me as much or as little as you want." He tilted his head toward her. "You know I will never repeat any of it. Not to your aunt, not to my mother."

Lissie tightened her navy blue cardigan around herself. "I don't know where to start."

"The beginning is a good place. I left, and you were sad. You must have met Alvan soon after."

She nodded, her mind drifting back in time. "A month. I went to a wedding with *Mam* and *Dat* in Maryland. I met him there." She shrugged. "He was nice enough to me." She looked at Menno. "He wasn't a bad person. I want you to know that. But he was weak and under the thumb of his parents. I saw that within hours of meeting him, but I hadn't heard from you. No one had and—" Her voice caught in her throat. "And I wanted to get away from Faith's Run, away from my memories of you. So when he asked me to marry him three days later, I said yes."

"You'd known him *three days*?" Menno shook his head. "Sorry. I shouldn't have said that. But I'm surprised your father gave his permission so quickly. And so soon after I left."

She sighed. "*Mam* was tired of hearing me cry. She wanted to be rid of me. I think they both did." She leaned back on the bench seat, contemplating her impulsiveness. Menno was right. How young and foolish she had been to accept Alvan's offer. "I married him two weeks later. I went with him and his parents to Ohio the day after the wedding."

"Oh, Lissie," Menno murmured.

"I know. It was all a blur then, still is," she said, shaking her head slowly. "Things were *oll recht* at first, I guess. We lived with his parents, which was like being a daughter in someone else's house. Alvan went to work each day, and I stayed home and cooked and cleaned at his mother's side." She pursed her mouth, thinking of her sour mother-in-law, who hadn't liked her the first time they met. "Alvan would have been fine with the arrangement for the rest of our lives, but when I was expecting Naomi, I insisted we move into our own place. His mother was so overbearing that I knew she wouldn't let me raise my children the way I saw fit."

Lissie was quiet for a moment, the memories drifting in her head. "He blamed me for our money troubles after that. He said it was my fault we never had anything. That we would have been fine if we had stayed with his parents. But I knew I couldn't raise children in that home. I had adapted to how strict they were, how old-fashioned, but there was no joy there. No conversation, no smiles, no laughter. I couldn't do it, Menno."

He turned right at a stop sign where they should have turned left to go home. "Understandable."

"Anyway, so we moved into a rental near his parents. But then Alvan lost his job, and we moved, and he lost another job, and we moved again. And it went on that way for the years we were married. Alvan worked in feed mills, sometimes country stores, stocking shelves, cutting meat. Whatever work he could find. He'd been trained as a mason, but he didn't like that work. He said he didn't like being outside in the heat or the cold." She groaned, bringing her hand to her forehead. "It was always something with Alvan. He didn't think people were fair to him, that the world wasn't fair to him. I tried to be supportive, but he could be harsh. He blamed me for all his troubles, real or not, and later he blamed our children."

She turned to Menno on the seat. "Should I be telling

you these things? Alvan was my husband and he's gone. Isn't it wrong to speak ill of the dead?"

"It's not like you're gossiping, Lissie. You're telling me what your life was like when we were apart. That helps us both."

She sighed, knowing he was right, but that didn't make it easier. "I always thought that being a parent came naturally, but Alvan never took to it. He didn't seem to feel that—" She looked at him, placing her hand on her chest. "That love I felt for my *kinner* when they took their first breath. You know what I mean." Her expression softened as her gaze met his. "I know you do. I see it in your eyes when you look at Daisy."

"I know exactly what you mean," he said softly. "I always heard folks speak of children as a gift from *Gott*, but I never understood it until I held Daisy in my arms that first time."

His words made her smile, but then she grew sober again. "I don't think Alvan loved Naomi and Jonah, though he enjoyed boasting about his son. He didn't give our boy the time of day at home, but he liked to talk big in front of others. He gave no mind to Naomi at all except to criticize or give orders."

She took a deep breath and exhaled, feeling herself relax. Somehow, as she spoke the words, the pain she carried in her heart seemed to ease. "I don't know when Alvan started drinking alcohol. Probably long before I noticed. It wasn't until he was fired from a good job at a butcher shop and we had to move in with his parents again that I realized something was causing him to act even worse than before." She stared straight ahead, watching the driving horse Clyde's ears twitch as a fly buzzed around his head. "I suspect Alvan was fired for drinking that last time. I also realize now that was why we never had as much money as I thought we should. He'd been drinking for years."

Lissie saw Menno tighten his hands into fists around the reins.

"I'm sorry. I'm upsetting you," she said.

"*Nay*, Alvan's who is upsetting me." He took a deep breath and slowly relaxed his hands. "Go on."

"Not much more to say. Alvan never worked again after losing the job at the butcher shop, though he was always gone, leaving the children and me with his mother. She was so terrible to us. Thinking back, I believe my husband did find work occasionally but kept the pay for himself."

"To buy alcohol."

She nodded, feeling a sense of peace as she neared the end of her story. "The night Alvan died, we'd had a terrible fight. He tried to hit Naomi. He'd slapped me before—"

Menno stiffened on the seat but said nothing.

"He'd never hit the children before, but that was my breaking point," she continued. "That night, I threatened to leave him and come home to Faith's Run. That made him angrier than I'd ever seen him. Not because he might lose us but because his parents would be upset. He was angry at me. At the children. At *Gott*. He stormed out of the house. Then I guess he went to the mailbox across the road. He accidentally stepped out in front of a truck. And he was gone," she said softly.

They were quiet for a quarter of a mile before Menno spoke, which was good for Lissie. She needed the time to rest her mind and her heart.

"Why didn't you come straight home after your husband passed, Lissie?"

She thought about the question before answering. "I don't know. I suppose I was grieving for the father of my children. For the life I had dreamed of. And I think a part of me was embarrassed. I didn't want to face everyone here."

"Embarrassed?" he said. "Why?"

She opened her eyes wide. "I don't know, Menno. Maybe over my foolish mistake in marrying a man I didn't know? Over the other bad choices I continued to make after that?"

He took her hand in his. "I'm so sorry all that happened to you, Lissie. I know I can't change the past. No one can do that. But we *can* make choices that give us the best chance at a good future. *Gott* willing."

She knew she should pull her hand away. But it felt good. So she didn't. "Let me guess. You think you could be a part of my future?" she said, feeling surprisingly lighthearted for all she had just relayed to him.

"I do," he said emphatically. "I love you, Lissie. And I want to marry you and be a father to your children. I want to spend the rest of my life making up for all the pain I caused you."

She shook her head. "*Nay*, I can't blame my troubles on you. I made those bad choices, Menno, and I alone."

"So make a good choice right now. Say you'll marry me. Or at least agree to walk out with me so I don't have to think of things to do and places to go where no one will see us together."

She laughed. "Annie says everyone already thinks we're a couple."

He pulled back at a four-way stop sign where no vehicles were in sight and turned to face her. "So let's not disappoint them."

Lissie covered her face with her hands. She didn't know what to say. What to do, and she was suddenly overwhelmed. And tired. It had been a long week.

"I'm sorry," Menno said when she didn't respond. "I don't want to pressure you. We don't have to talk about this anymore tonight. You need time to think and that's *okey*. I'm not going anywhere, Lissie. Not unless you boot me off the property."

She lowered her hands, frowning at him. "I can't *kick* you off your own property."

"It's not mine. Well, won't be soon. I'm deeding it to you. There'll be some papers to sign, but it will be yours. Both houses and the hundred and ten acres."

Overcome by emotion, Lissie's breath caught in her throat. "Menno—"

"No argument, Lissie. No matter what happens between us, I need to know that you, Eunice, Naomi and Jonah have a place of your own. I don't want you to ever have to rent again. You grew up there and your children deserve the same."

Her heart thumped. "Menno, I can never pay you—"

"I know I can never make up for what I did to you, but I need you to let me do this. *Gott* has blessed me with a healthy business. I want to do this." It was dark now, but she could see him grin. "And I'm praying that Daisy and I'll live in the big house with you one day. Then whose name is on the paperwork won't matter."

She clasped her hands and gulped. And instead of arguing further, she whispered, "*Danki*, Menno."

"Thank you for letting me do this for you. For your

family. Now, are you ready to go home?" he asked, his voice a caress.

"I am." Lissie didn't know what made her do it, but she reached for him. And then they rode the rest of the way home in comfortable silence, still holding hands.

Chapter Thirteen

Thankfully, when Lissie said goodbye to Menno and entered the house, Eunice had already sent the children upstairs to put on their pajamas. Lissie prayed with Naomi and Jonah, and they got into bed without protest. Having had a wonderful day, they whispered excitedly about the next school year as Lissie closed their door.

Standing in the dark hall, she heard Eunice below in the kitchen. She considered going directly to bed because if she went downstairs, her aunt would surely grill her about what was happening between her and Menno. Lissie wasn't ready to have that conversation because she didn't know. A part of her wanted to walk across the driveway and tell Menno she would marry him. She loved him. She had never stopped loving him; no matter how she tried to deny it, she knew it in her heart.

So why was she hesitating to accept his love? His offer of marriage?

The sound of breaking glass below startled Lissie, and she hurried downstairs. "Eunice?" She hurried into the kitchen to find her aunt stooping to pick up bits of clear glass from the floor.

"*Ach*, all's well. Just me being clumsy. I broke a glass,"

her aunt said. "It was sitting on the edge of the counter, I bumped it, and down it went."

"I'll get the broom." Lissie returned from the pantry, and they cleaned up the glass together.

"Children asleep?" Eunice asked, walking to the sink to finish washing a bowl they'd used to take chowchow to the school supper.

"If they aren't, they soon will be." Lissie leaned over the table to adjust the wick on the kerosene lamp her aunt had lit. "It was sweet of Menno to take them with him and Daisy to the school this morning to help with the barbecue. He wore them out, keeping them out all day."

Eunice cut her eyes at Lissie. "He is sweet, that one."

"He is," Lissie murmured, thinking about how nice it had been to ride home beside him, sitting closer than she probably should have. With a dish towel in hand, Lissie took the serving bowl from the wooden dish rack. Despite her difficult discussion with Menno, she wished the trip had been longer. Yet she felt guilty for that. Her husband had only been gone a year. Was it right to have these feelings for Menno, the kind she had never had for Alvan?

Eunice watched Lissie, her eyes sharp behind the smudged lenses of her eyeglasses. "Sometimes it's good to speak the things you're thinking. Helps sort the grain from the chaff," she said gently.

When Lissie opened her mouth, she intended to say that she had nothing to talk about, but the words spilled out before she could stop them. She told her *endie* everything. She explained how the weeks of treating Menno like a friend had allowed her to get to know him again. She told her aunt what Annie Fischer and Elzy Shroder had said, about Menno saying he loved her and wanted to marry her, and about him deeding her the farm. She even admitted that she still loved him and was tempted to agree to marry him.

Lissie was so caught up in lightening the burdens of her heart and mind that she didn't remember sitting at the kitchen table. She had no recollection of how the cup of tea ended up in front of her. After saying everything she needed to, she sat back in her chair, more exhausted than she remembered being in a long time. "I don't know what to do, *Endie*," she murmured. Making fists, she pressed the heels of her hands to her forehead. "One minute I'm scared and confused. The next, my heart is beating fast and all I want is to be with him. I don't know what's wrong with me." She gave a humorless chuckle. "It feels worse than when we were teenagers."

Eunice laughed; her gravelly voice filled with pure joy. "*Ach*. To be young again." She slurped her tea and nodded thoughtfully. "I have a question for you."

"Ya?" Lissie wrapped her hands around the warm mug, inhaling the soothing scent of her peppermint tea.

"How important is your faith to you? And I don't mean the easy things like going to church, covering your hair, or not wearing a red dress." She tapped her chest. "I mean here, in your heart. How strong is your faith? Do you believe the word of *Gott*?"

Lissie clasped her hands, thinking before she spoke, because faith was something she knew had to be examined regularly. It had to be nurtured. There had been times in her life—difficult times with Alvan—when she had felt her faith fading. Returning to Faith's Run had not only restored her faith but also revitalized it. "It means everything to me," she said, calm but passionate. "My faith makes me who I am. It's what guides me every day."

"Then it's time to let go of your anger with Menno and

truly forgive him. That burden is yours now because *Gott* has already forgiven him and the boy has forgiven himself. You think you can do that?"

Lissie stared into her mug. "I've been working on that and I think… I think that spending time with him has helped me forgive him. But I haven't forgotten." Tears suddenly filled her eyes. "It was Menno's fault I married a man I didn't know. What will ever make me forget the one thing that happened in my life that turned it upside down?"

Her aunt smiled, wisdom in her soft expression. "Time," she answered. "And happiness. And community. And *Gott.* With enough time, most things in our pasts are forgotten or faded until we're no longer certain the memory is real. As a woman who has been blessed to live more than eight decades, this is one thing I can tell you for sure and certain."

Lissie took a deep, shuddering breath and reached for her mug but didn't drink.

"I've another question for you," Eunice pressed. "And then I'll let you be."

"What's that?" Lissie met her aunt's gaze.

"Now I want complete honesty, *ya*?"

Lissie nodded.

Eunice hesitated and said, "You said you still have feelings for Menno."

Lissie nodded, afraid that if she said it out loud, she'd cry in earnest.

"Then what's holding you back?" Eunice asked.

"I don't know." Lissie raised her hands and let them fall to her lap. "I've made so many mistakes that I'm afraid to trust myself. Accepting Alvan's proposal was a terrible idea. I knew it a week after the marriage. I wed him impulsively after Menno left me, and Alvan turned out to be the biggest mistake of my life." She looked upward, silently asking *Gott*'s forgiveness for saying such a thing about the father of her children. She returned her gaze to Eunice's. "If I choose Menno, how will I know it's the right thing to do?"

Her aunt leaned closer. "Menno is not Alvan."

"*Nay*, he is not," she agreed.

"So why not give Menno a chance. Set aside your anger, your fear, your bitterness over the past and consider him for the man he is now, not the boy he was a decade ago." Eunice smiled mischievously. "You're overthinking this. Have some fun, Lissie. Enjoy Menno's company. See if the spark is still there." She poked her with an arthritic finger. "Because you deserve to be happy. And you deserve to be loved like I know Menno loves you."

Lissie gave what her aunt had just said a long moment of thought. "I do deserve to be loved, don't I?" she murmured.

"You do." Eunice downed the last of her tea and rose, her chair sliding loudly across the hardwood floor. "Now to bed with you. See what the new day brings."

Menno leaned on the big oak reception desk opposite where Lissie sat writing in his mother's appointment book. "You ready? This lunch isn't going to eat itself." He lifted the picnic basket to show her.

Over the past couple of weeks, it had become a habit for them to have lunch several times a week, depending on her schedule at the office. After their conversation on the night of the school barbecue, Lissie's demeanor had changed. She'd gradually stopped treating him like a friend and started to treat him more like a beau. While they had not publicly declared they were seeing each other, she no longer argued with people who referred to them as a couple. Although she hadn't yet admitted she still loved him, she allowed him to openly proclaim his love for her. Menno was sure it would only be a matter of time before she brought up the subject of her feelings for him and marriage. And while he'd marry her today, he would let her decide when that would happen, giving her as much time as she needed.

"Lissie." Menno glanced at the big black-and-white clock on the wall behind her. "You said the next client would be here at one."

She glanced up at the clock, pushing a stray tendril of nutmeg-colored hair behind her ear. "Oh, dear, how did it get so late already?"

"It's how time works," he teased. He didn't know how it was possible, but she seemed to get prettier every day. He couldn't believe that after all these years of dreaming of a life with her, it might come to be. And he thanked *Gott* every day for it. "It works that way. Especially in an office where there's always more work than can be done in a day." He set the basket on the desk and plucked the pen from her hand.

"Menno!" She laughed bashfully as if they were eighteen and nineteen again as she rose and let him wrap his arms around her. "Someone will see us!"

"Who? There's no one here but *Mam*, and I think she already knows what's up with the two of us. She spotted us holding hands under the table when we all came for supper the other night."

"Still, it's not seemly," she admonished.

But her protests were half-hearted, and he held her a

moment longer before releasing her. "Hungry?" he asked, retrieving the picnic basket.

"Starving."

He led her out the door to the office parking lot. "Where shall we eat today? By the pond? In the orchard? The picnic table under the maples?"

She walked beside him, the hem of her blue dress brushing against his pant leg. His grandmother had made several new dresses for her, and it was nice to see her in something that didn't look like it belonged in the rag bag. While it wasn't the Amish way to have closets full of clothing, when she became his wife, he would see to it that she and her children never had to wear hand-me-downs again.

"Hmm." She tilted her head to look at him. "The picnic table, I think. Where it's shady."

Her smile lit up her face, and how she looked at him made him feel lightheaded. If this woman married him, all the trials and tribulations of his past would have been worth it. "Sounds good."

They were soon seated side by side at the picnic table, with the spread he'd packed laid out on a square of curtain remnant from his basket.

"*Ach*, you made these stuffed eggs?" Lissie asked, eating half of one in two bites. "They're so good."

"Daisy and I made them." He grimaced. "But be careful. There could be shells. I let her peel the eggs."

Lissie picked up one of the cloth napkins he'd packed. "What's in them? They're spicy, but not too hot. And cheesy. How do you even know how to make something like this?"

"That's salsa and cheddar cheese." He stuffed half an egg into his mouth and chewed. "And some sour cream mixed in with the mayo. Something I learned to make back in my Englisher days." He chuckled. "It was the only thing Heather could make that wasn't out of a can or a box."

The moment the words came out of his mouth, he regretted them. What was wrong with him, bringing up the name of the woman he'd had a child with when he was so close to having the love of his life agree to marry him?

He looked at her. "I'm sorry. I shouldn't have—" He struggled to find the right words. "I didn't mean to bring her up."

"It's *oll recht*, Menno." Lissie picked up the bottle of orange soda he'd opened for her and took a sip. "I don't mind."

"You don't?" Relief washed over him.

"You said you don't mind when I bring up Alvan."

"I don't. He's part of your past," he said carefully. The truth was that he sometimes had to grit his teeth when she spoke the man's name, but that was because of how he had treated Lissie and the children, not jealousy. "He's Naomi and Jonah's father. Always will be. Though I hope I can be a father to them too, someday."

She smiled with understanding and held out the bottle. "A sip?"

He nodded, accepting it. "I suppose you'll want some of my root beer, too?"

"I do." She picked up his bottle and, smiling at each other, their gazes locked, they both sampled the soda.

Menno then started pulling out the other things he brought for lunch as they discussed various housekeeping topics, as his mother liked to call them. He would drop Eunice's harness off for repair. She would oversee Daisy picking out the cloth for two dresses her grandmother was making for her. They would walk to church on Sunday because they preferred to walk when the weather permitted, but would send Jonah with Eunice in the buggy because he was recovering from a bad case of poison ivy after chasing a squirrel into a patch at the edge of the woods.

Lissie placed a piece of cheddar cheese on a cracker. "Your *mam* wants me to work Monday. Rose has a new beau and asked for the day off so she could go with him and meet his *grossmammi*," she said, opening her eyes wide.

"Good for her." Perhaps she'd leave him alone if things worked out with the beau.

"But Jonah and Naomi both had dental appointments Monday at ten and I hate to reschedule." She handed him the cracker with cheddar on top. "I already hired a driver. I hate to ask, but is there any way you could take them?"

"I'm glad you feel like you can ask." He accepted the cracker. "*Ya*, I can take them. That'll work perfectly because I need to go to Sam's Club for paper goods for the shop. We're almost out of spoons and napkins, and I imagine we'll be busy next week with the new flavor coming out."

"*Danki*," she said, eating an apple slice. "Oh, and I need to go to Byler's for groceries Saturday, and I know you like to shop on Saturdays. Want to go together? No need for both of us to drive separately. I'm sure the *kinner* will be happy to ride along." She hesitated. "Unless you need to be at your shop."

He dismissed her suggestion with a wave of his hand. He'd go to the moon with her if she asked. "I don't need to be there Saturday. My new manager's working out well. He doesn't need me looking over his shoulder. But I have a better idea. When we were over for supper, *Mam* said something about having the girls over on Saturday. She worries she doesn't spend enough time with her grandchildren. We can send Jonah with them. He can tag along with Jude in the cow barn in his new boots."

When Menno looked up at Lissie, he was startled to see her dark eyes brimming with tears…yet she was smiling. Women were such a mystery to him. "What?" he asked. "Did I say something wrong?"

She shook her head, laughing as she blotted her eyes with her napkin. "Nothing, it's just—" She sniffed. "Elizabeth calling my children her grandchildren—it makes them so happy. They love your *mam*."

"And she loves them." He leaned closer. "Of course, if you marry me, she *will* be their grandmother."

"Menno!" Lissie chastised, motioning for him to stop.

"I know. I know. Don't push you. I just wanted to remind you that the offer is still open," he teased.

She laughed, unwrapping two cookies from a piece of waxed cloth and handing him one. "As if I could forget. You don't let a day go by that you don't remind me the *offer's still open*."

"Not *every* day," he said, laughing with her.

She handed him one of the big lemon cookies. "Every day, Menno." She gestured with her cookie as she rose from the bench. "I just saw a buggy pull in. I'd best get back to work. So, it's settled? Grocery shopping at Byler's on Saturday. And maybe we could go to Redner's too?"

He swung his legs around and stood up from the picnic table. "Wherever you like. Should I hire a driver? Saturdays are busy in town. The traffic's heavy, and the English never seem to be looking where they're going."

"I'd rather take the wagon if you're okay with that." They were standing close together and she smiled up at him. "The ride in and out of town is longer. More time to be alone together."

Menno's heart swelled as he gazed into her brown eyes. The way Lissie was looking at him, he might be a married man by harvest.

On Saturday morning, Menno pulled into the large parking lot and slowly made his way to the far end, where there was a single hitching post. They decided it would be wise to visit the larger Englisher grocery store before it got too busy, but the parking lot was already crowded with cars, and motor vehicles sped by on the main road just beyond the hitching post.

"Maybe this wasn't such a good idea," Lissie said, climbing down from the wagon as she watched a small red car and a big black SUV try to pull into the same parking spot simultaneously. When neither could get into the space, both drivers honked their horns.

Menno walked to the hitching post and tied the horse securely. Thankfully, the thoroughbred wasn't skittish. "We'll be fine." He rested his hand on the horse's neck. "Won't we, Clyde?"

Lissie frowned, watching as cars pulled into parking spaces to exit while an unattended cart slowly rolled across the lot and struck the tailgate of a white pickup. "Places like this worry me," she fretted. "So many cars. So much confusion."

They started across the huge lot. "It's perfectly safe, Lissie." He looked around. "Looks like a typical Saturday morning at the grocery store to me."

She glanced at him. He wore his flat-brimmed straw hat and Ray-Ban sunglasses. She had just cut his blond hair that morning, and he looked handsome in a pale green shirt, broadcloth pants and leather suspenders. "Says the man who used to drive a truck."

He laughed. "Would it make you feel better if I held your hand?"

His hand brushed against hers. She knew he was teasing, knowing it wasn't proper in public, but she wanted to hold it. She pushed him away playfully. Things had changed between them since their talk that night on the way home from the school. For all intents and purposes, they were courting. It was only a matter of time before she would tell him she loved him, too. And then it would be time to take the next step. But she wasn't ready to think about marriage. Not yet.

"I don't need anyone to hold my hand, Menno. I'll be—*Ach*," she groaned, looking over her shoulder at the wagon in the distance behind them. "I forgot my shopping bags."

"I'll get them." He turned to go, but she caught his arm.

"*Nay*, I'll do it. You get a cart."

"*Okey*," he said.

She walked in the opposite direction. At the wagon, as she reached under the seat to retrieve her reusable cloth bags, she heard the screech of tires, immediately followed by a bump. As she turned to look toward the commotion, she heard a woman scream.

The first thing Lissie saw was the big white car stopped sideways in the lane between two rows of cars. Then she saw an Amish hat and fancy sunglasses on the pavement. She dropped the shopping bags and took off running.

Chapter Fourteen

The white car couldn't have been more than fifty feet from Lissie, but it felt like it took her a lifetime to reach it. Suddenly, there were Englishers in cutoff denim shorts, tank tops and flowered shirts everywhere. They gawked and shouted.

A man exited the white car, leaving his door open. "I didn't see him," he cried in anguish. "I never saw him."

Lissie found Menno lying on his back on the pavement behind the vehicle, his eyes closed and his arms spread wide. She dropped to her knees, and the heat of the blacktop burned her skin. "My love," she murmured under her breath. Heart pounding, she surveyed him from his boots to his bare head. No limbs appeared to be broken, and his chest rose and fell. He was alive, thank *Gott*! Voices bombarded her from every direction as shoppers moved around them.

"Someone call 911!" someone shouted in a booming voice.

"Is he *Aimish*? I think he's *Aimish*," said another.

"The old guy just backed right over him!"

Blocking out the voices, Lissie gently pressed her hand to Menno's smooth, shaven cheek. "Menno? Can you hear me?"

Out of the corner of her eye, she saw blood blooming on the back of his head, staining his golden hair. "Menno, please," she choked, tears running down her cheeks as she fought panic. *She couldn't lose him again. She wouldn't.* "Menno, open your eyes. Please," she begged in Pennsylvania *Deitsch*. "You have to wake up so I can tell you I love you. So I can tell you I'll marry you. Talk to me. Tell me about our wedding. When shall we marry? Who will stand as our witnesses?"

"Back up, everyone," a woman said loudly. "I'm a paramedic. Give us some room and make sure no one tries to move any of these cars. Did someone call 911?"

"I called!" a woman answered.

Lissie felt someone kneel beside her.

"Is this your husband?"

Lissie looked over to see a woman about her age in a blue uniform with dark hair styled in tiny braids all over her head. She lowered a red bag from her shoulder to the ground beside Menno. "Is this your husband?" the woman repeated.

Menno had begun to rouse, and Lissie shifted her gaze to him. "My…my fiancé," she said in English.

"I'm Whitney and I'm a paramedic. I was going by when I heard all the fuss," she explained as she studied him. "What's his name?"

"Menno Bontrager," Lissie choked, watching as he moved one hand, then a leg.

"Menno," the paramedic said as she took his pulse. "Can you open your eyes for me?"

"Menno," Lissie cried. "She's a paramedic and she's here to help you."

Menno's eyelids flickered and he brought his hand to his chest.

"There we go," Whitney said as Menno opened his eyes, then squinted. "I know. Bright out here, right?"

"Menno," Lissie cried, gazing into his bright blue eyes. *"Ach, danki, Gott."*

He tried to turn his head to look at Lissie, but the paramedic laid her hand on his chest again. "Menno, I need you to lie still until I can make sure you're okay." She glanced at Lissie. "How long was he out?"

Lissie blinked, not sure what she meant.

"Unconscious," Whitney said. "A minute? Two?"

"I don't know," Lissie said. "Not long. I heard a sound and then I saw the car and his hat and I ran. From our wagon over there." She pointed to the southeast corner of the parking lot.

"Lissie," Menno said, blinking repeatedly. "What happened?"

She moved to his other side so she wouldn't be in the way as the woman fastened a blood pressure cuff on his arm.

"Looks like you've got a bit of a bump on your head there, Menno." Whitney's tone was reassuring in its casualness. "I'll have a look at that in a sec."

Lissie gazed into Menno's eyes, relief bringing another rush of tears. "Someone backed into you. A car."

The sound of a siren filled the morning air.

"That was quick," Whitney said. She looked at Lissie, then at Menno. "My colleagues are just pulling in. So, here's what's going to happen. Once they arrive, I'll pass you on to them. They'll have a look at you, and then you'll be taken by ambulance to the hospital."

"I'm fine. I don't need to go to the hospital," Menno said, groggy. He tried to sit up but swayed.

Lissie and the paramedic grabbed his shoulders to steady and ease him back.

"Let's just chill right here, Menno." Whitney eyed the growing blood spot in his hair. "You've got a nice bump on your head."

"I'm fine," he repeated, but then he closed his eyes again.

"I think you probably are fine," Whitney said. "But I think your head hit the pavement pretty hard, and since you were out for a minute or so, a scan might be in order."

Menno groaned. "I don't need a scan. I'm supposed to get groceries and—"

"Hush," Lissie said softly, leaning closer to him. "You're going to the hospital."

"Hey," Whitney called, getting to her feet as a man in a van marked *Paramedics* exited the vehicle. She walked away.

Lissie returned her attention to Menno, grateful that Whitney insisted he go to the hospital. He had closed his eyes again, and she feared he was hurt worse than he appeared. What if he had a brain injury?

Please, Gott, she prayed. *Let Menno be all right.*

"Lissie?" Menno said, his eyes closed.

She leaned closer, taking his hand. "I'm right here."

"I thought I heard you say something," he said dreamily.

"What was that?" she breathed.

He opened his eyes. "You said you loved me. You said you'd marry me." He smiled a lopsided grin. "Did you say that, or was I dreaming?"

"I did say it," she said, fighting tears again. Only this time, they were tears of joy because she knew he would be all right. "I was afraid I lost you, Menno. I don't want to lose you again."

He held her gaze. "Then say it again," he whispered.

"Say what?" she teased, knowing full well what he meant.

"Tell me you love me, Lissie. Tell me that you'll marry me."

A tear slipped down her cheek. "I love you and I want to marry you, Menno. I'd marry you today if I could."

He squeezed her hand as his eyes grew moist. "I'll speak with the bishop tomorrow."

Panting from exertion, Lissie walked off the volleyball court in the Bontragers' backyard as Menno's brother Asher substituted for her. "I'm out," she announced, looking at Menno, who was playing for the other team. "When this game is over, I think it's time to call it a night."

"Nooo," Daisy, Naomi and Junia cried in unison from the far side of the grassy court, their protests bordering on whining.

"We want to play again with the cousins!" Junia called.

Menno met Lissie's gaze and turned to speak to the girls. "There'll be time for playing tomorrow, after the ceremony." Someone tossed the volleyball to him, and he hit it over the net to Asher to serve. "It's time to head up to the house," he told the girls. "Tomorrow's going to be a long day."

"Can't we watch the end of the game, *Dat*?" Daisy begged. "Pleeeease?"

Menno glanced at Lissie and she nodded. "But then it's off to bed with all of you," he warned.

"Won't take long. Two points and we win," Asher

called good-naturedly. He was the spitting image of Menno: handsome, blond hair, blue eyes.

Lissie didn't hear Menno's comeback as she walked away, but everyone laughed.

Instead of joining one of the clusters of out-of-town guests, Lissie settled beneath a tree festooned with twinkling solar lights intended for the next day. Although it wasn't dark yet, the setting sun could no longer penetrate the lush branches of the silver maple, causing the lights to shimmer like fireflies.

Settling into the grass, she leaned back against the massive tree trunk, stretching out her legs so that her dirty bare feet poked out from beneath the hem of her dress. She knew she should socialize with their guests, many of whom had traveled from as far as Canada, but she needed a moment to herself.

After Menno's accident, the days had flown by like daisy petals caught in the wind. So much had happened in the last six weeks that it made her head spin. Following a CT scan, it was determined that he had a concussion, in addition to the small laceration on his head, which required six stitches. He was sent home with advice to take it easy for a few days and see his primary care doctor the following week. Despite having his head bandaged and Lissie begging him to stay home from church the next day, Menno kept the promise he'd made to her from the pavement of the grocery store parking lot. He spoke to their bishop and made an appointment to discuss getting his approval for their marriage. Bishop Hamul was full of questions during their first visit as a betrothed couple but gave his blessing. Due to their age and past, they agreed there was no need to wait until fall, when most weddings took place in Faith's Run, and suddenly Lissie had a wedding to plan.

After several discussions, Menno and Lissie accepted his mother's offer to host the wedding. Ultimately, it made more sense. Her home was more than twice the size of the one Lissie now legally owned, which meant Elizabeth had more room to accommodate out-of-town guests, and a kitchen and yard that were much better suited for their "small" wedding of one hundred and twenty-five guests.

With the sounds of the volleyball game still ongoing, Lissie glanced toward the huge white tent that Elizabeth had insisted on renting at her own expense. The tent had been set up that morning with tables and chairs, as well as the *eck* where she and Menno would sit for the lunch and supper that would be served. The tent would keep the guests cool in the August sun while also preventing them from getting wet should a summer shower pass through. Lissie's new friend Annie, who was only eight weeks postpartum from having her twins, had taken on the task of decorating the tent. As Lissie gazed at it now, with the tables covered in blue cloth and adorned with multicolored mason jars of wildflowers and yards of tulle, her heart suddenly hammered in her chest. The finality of the following day settled on her.

She was getting married. *Tomorrow.*

She was marrying Menno. And she would be married to him until death.

She swallowed hard as she watched the volleyball players disperse, everyone laughing and talking. Her gaze fell on Menno walking to where his little sister, daughter and Naomi stood with several other girls who were overnight guests. Naomi and Jonah would stay with the Bontragers for the night, as would Menno and Daisy, to give the bride some privacy to prepare for the ceremony and festivities. Her aunt, tired from long days of cooking and cleaning with Sheba for the big day, had already left for home in the buggy. Lissie would take one of the family's push scooters home. In the morning, she would dress in the traditional long-sleeve tab dress that Sheba had made, and Eunice would drive her back at nine for the private ceremony inside. That would be followed by a church service under the big tent, and lunch would be served.

Lissie's mouth felt dry.

Tomorrow she would be a wife again.

The prospect terrified her. She had tried to be a good wife to Alvan, but had she truly succeeded? He didn't believe so and had told her more times than she could count. What if she couldn't be a good wife to Menno either? Impulsiveness had led her to wedding vows once before. Was agreeing to marry Menno after his accident yet another instance of a rash decision that would prove to be a mistake?

Lissie rose, clutching the trunk of the tree for support. The gathering was breaking up. People who had traveled from nearby or were staying in Faith's Run with friends headed to their buggies, waving and saying their goodbyes. She forced a smile as she waved repeatedly, her voice catching in her throat as she returned good-nights and thanked them for their well-wishes. She knew she should see them off, but felt like her bare feet were glued to the ground.

Jonah, Naomi and Daisy ran across the volleyball field to her. Thankfully, they were too excited about the sleepover with children their own age to notice how upset she was when they said good-night. She kissed each one on the top of the head, nearly choking on stifled tears when Daisy ran back for another hug before joining the other children heading back to the house.

If Lissie married Menno and it turned out to be a mistake, she wouldn't just ruin his life, but also that of his sweet daughter. Lissie loved Daisy as much as she loved her own children. She could no more intentionally hurt the little girl than she could her own *kinner*. And what about Naomi and Jonah? How would they be affected if this marriage proved to be a bad idea?

She squeezed her eyes shut, willing herself not to cry. Why had she been so quick to tell Menno she would marry him? Why hadn't she given it more thought and time?

"I can't do this," Lissie said to herself, trembling. *I didn't think this through. Menno was hurt, and I was scared, and I had agreed to marry him on the spur of the moment. Just like I did with Alvan. I was hurting after Menno left me, and when Alvan asked me to marry him, I just said yes.*

From beneath the tree, she watched Menno call goodnight to the children again, as well as a few others. Then, alone, he turned to look for her.

Lissie shook with emotion. She could not allow her rash behavior to cause harm to others. She *would* not do it to Menno. She loved him too much.

Lissie walked toward the lane.

"Lissie!" Menno called.

She saw him start toward her, but one of his father's cousins spoke to him and he turned back.

Grabbing her sneakers from the grass, Lissie hurried toward a hitching post where she had seen several push scooters earlier in the day. There were at least half a dozen on the farm, and anyone in the family who wanted to use one could. Thankful to have avoided any lingering guests, she stopped to slip into her sneakers and grabbed the closest scooter. Behind her, she heard Menno call her name, but she continued along the grass beside the gravel lane. Riding on the bumpy surface was too difficult, but once she reached the road, she would hop on and be home in no time. Once home, she would climb into bed, pull the sheet over her head and sleep. There would be time enough in the morning to cancel the wedding. She had almost done it the morning she married Alvan. This time, she would find the strength to do it.

Lissie almost reached the road before she heard pounding feet and Menno appeared at her side. She kept walking.

"Lissie, *mein liebs*." He was breathing hard from running as he fell into step beside her. "You're going home? And you didn't say goodbye?" He chuckled, sounding nervous. "You know, that's a good way to worry a man the night before their wedding."

She continued pushing the scooter and said nothing.

"Are you *oll recht*? You must be exhausted. I'm sorry. We should have sent everyone home sooner, but we were having such a good time and—" He grabbed her arm, halting.

Tears filled her eyes, and she couldn't bear to look at him as she stood there. The sun was setting, casting long shadows across the driveway. Menno's ice cream shop stood not far in the distance, and she focused on the whitewashed building. Though it was closed, she spotted an Amish man leaning against the side. From this distance, she couldn't tell who he was.

Lissie stiffened as Menno gripped her arm tighter, and he dropped his hand. "Did I say something wrong? I'm sorry. Was it what I said about how you served the volleyball? I was just teasing, Lissie. Englishers call it talking trash. I didn't mean—"

"I can't marry you," she blurted, feeling as if she would explode if she didn't say it out loud.

"What?" He sounded stunned. Confused.

She swallowed hard, placing her right foot on the scooter so she could push off with her left. "I said I can't—" Her voice caught in her throat, and tears filled her eyes. She wanted to marry Menno more than anything in this earthly world, but she wouldn't. She knew he'd be hurt, but he'd recover. Hurting him now was better than a lifetime of hurting him, wasn't it?

"I changed my mind. I'm not marrying you."

"You're not—" Suddenly, his tone changed. He no longer sounded hurt; he sounded angry. "You're not going to marry me?" He paused and then said stiffly, "Why?"

"Because I'm not," she answered. Then she pushed off hard, rolling across the last few feet of bumpy gravel before she hit the pavement and leaned into the turn for home.

Menno didn't follow her, and for that, she was grateful.

Chapter Fifteen

Heart pounding, Menno stood at the end of his mother's lane and watched the love of his life ride away. He clenched his fist at his side, a lump rising in his throat. His gaze followed Lissie as she grew smaller, the flutter of her blue dress mesmerizing him. *She doesn't want to marry me. She's changed her mind. In her eyes, I'm not worthy of her love.* He was still standing there dumbly when his brother came to him.

Disoriented, Menno looked up, wondering where Jude had come from. "I thought you were walking Lydia Miller home."

Jude slid his hands into his pockets. A long blade of grass poked from his mouth, bobbing up and down as he spoke. "I thought I was, too. She just wanted to ask if I knew if Asher was seeing anyone."

"*Our* Asher? He's a teenager."

"Our brother turned twenty on his last birthday. Plenty old enough to catch a pretty girl like Lydia's eye."

Menno grimaced and shook his head. "Sorry, Jude."

Jude shrugged and lifted his chin toward the road. "What was that all about? Lissie tearing off like that." The blade of grass between his lips continued to bob.

Emotion welled in Menno's throat and his words came

out thickly. "She says she changed her mind. She told me—" His voice caught in his throat and he wiped his eyes with the back of his hand. He wouldn't cry in front of his little brother. "She doesn't want to marry me."

Jude plucked the grass from his mouth and tossed it. "She said she didn't want to marry you?" he questioned, sounding as shocked as Menno. "Now she's saying this? The night before you wed?" When Menno didn't answer, he said, "She say why?"

Menno lowered his head and scuffed his boot, kicking up bits of gravel as he shook his head no. He was so devastated that his heart ached in his chest. He couldn't believe Lissie was doing this, after all they'd been through. After all it had taken for them to get to this point. All the pain they had suffered together, the loneliness, the sense of hopelessness. Suddenly, a thought struck him, and he snapped his head up. "What if she did this on purpose? What if this was her plan all along?"

"What?" Jude's tone was incredulous.

Menno had choked on his last words, and it took him a moment to go on. "What if Lissie came here intending to pretend to fall in love with me and agreeing to marry me so that she could back out at the last minute?"

Jude scowled. "That makes no sense, *bruder.* Why would she do that?"

"To get back at me," Menno answered bitterly. "For leaving her."

"That's ridiculous." Jude scoffed, batting at a buzzing mosquito. "She didn't even know you were here."

"Maybe she lied about that."

"Lissie? Lie?" Jude cocked his head. "You sure there's no permanent damage from that accident?"

Menno ignored his brother's sarcastic remark. He felt

as if he were falling from a great height. He couldn't catch his breath, and he was lightheaded. How could Lissie have betrayed him like this? How could she have— "Maybe," he continued. "Maybe this was her plan all along."

"Menno, listen to yourself." Jude stepped in front of him, grabbing his shoulders and shaking him. "You don't believe any of this, do you? Lissie loves you. I envy the way she looks at you." He shook his head adamantly. "No, there's something else going on here. Maybe she just has cold feet. You hear people talk about that all the time. Being scared the night before you promise your life to another is normal. I know I would be."

Menno lowered his head, his brother still holding him. "Do you think so?"

"I know so."

"And what do you know about a woman's heart?" Menno pulled away and took his handkerchief from his pocket. He wiped his nose with it. Jude's words penetrated the wall of crazy ideas his mind was building. He knew Lissie as well as he knew himself. She didn't have a mean bone in her body. She would never do such an awful thing to him. She would never hurt anyone on purpose. He sniffed again. "You think she wants to marry me…and is just scared?"

"From the few things she's said, what others have said, it sounds like she had a pretty hard life with her husband. How could she not be scared?"

Menno took a deep breath and stuffed his handkerchief back into his pocket. "But this is me. I've loved her since we were kids. This is all I've ever wanted. I've been praying for this since I was a kid."

"Don't let this be the end of it. Don't think the worst of the woman you love without an explanation." He hesitated. "I know it's not your way, but you should fight for her."

"You're right." Menno laid his hand over his eyes. "What was I thinking? This is Lissie. My Lissie. We've been talking for months about the life we'll have together. She chose a color for me to paint the pantry next week." He looked up. "A woman doesn't choose a paint color and buy a man a nice brush if she doesn't intend to have him paint for her, does she?"

Jude chuckled dryly. "I'm not saying I know *that* much about women."

Menno managed a smile and for a moment he felt ashamed that he had thought such a terrible thing of Lissie, even for a moment. He met his brother's gaze. "I should go to her."

Jude raised an eyebrow. "*You think*?"

Menno turned to head back up the driveway. "I'll hitch the wagon."

"That'll take too much time. Why don't you take a push scooter? It'll be faster than getting Clyde out of the pasture and harnessing up."

Menno spun back around. "Good point. I'll grab one from the barn."

Jude pointed to the ice cream shop that was hardly visible now that twilight had turned to night. "There's one behind the barn. The big green one. The one with the battery lights." When Menno looked at him questioningly, he sheepishly added, "I was hoping to take Lydia for a ride."

"Good idea." Menno pointed at him as he started for the ice cream shop. "Thanks, *bruder*." He patted Jude on the back as he passed him.

Jude turned to watch him go. "If you hurry, you might even be able to catch up with her."

"I don't know about that. She seemed pretty determined when she left here," Menno returned, hope swelling in his chest with every step he took. "But I'm sure going to try."

Menno managed to catch up with Lissie as she reached her back porch. She must have been flying down the road. She darted for the door when she saw him coming up the driveway. He leaped off the push scooter, dropping it into the grass, and ran the final distance. "We need to talk."

"I don't want to talk to you," Lissie retorted firmly, turning her back to him. "Not tonight, Menno." She opened the door, stepped inside and slammed it.

"Lissie, please!" He hurried up the steps.

"I don't want to talk to you," she repeated. He could hear that she was crying. "I don't want to see you. Go home."

Frustrated, he grabbed the doorknob. Normally, he wasn't the kind of man to force his way into a place he wasn't wanted. But these weren't ordinary circumstances. "Lissie, I'm coming in."

"No, you're not."

Before he could turn the doorknob, he heard a loud click. "Oh, you did not," he muttered to himself. "You did not just lock me out."

He tried the knob anyway. It wouldn't turn.

"Lissie!" He made a fist and swung it at the door, but at the last second, he opened his hand so that he struck it with his palm.

"Don't you bang on my door!" she shouted. "You're going to wake up Eunice."

He might have laughed in another situation. "And you

think hollering at me like that isn't going to wake her?" he asked.

"I am not—" She must have realized that she *was* shouting because she went quiet for a moment and then more softly said, "Please, Menno. I really can't do this tonight. No matter what you say, you won't change my mind. I meant it when I said there will be no wedding tomorrow."

He hesitated briefly, thinking about what his brother had said. About how scary this must be for her, especially after what she'd been through with Alvan. Menno and Lissie had talked quite a bit about her husband in the past couple of weeks. She'd told him things about Alvan's treatment of her that had made his blood boil. Of course she would be afraid to marry again. Now that he had calmed down, he wondered how he could have been so foolish as to not expect Lissie to drag her feet at the last moment.

He rested his forehead and hand on the door. "Lissie, I'm not here to try to change your mind," he said, hearing a faint tremor in his voice. Of course, he hoped he could change her mind, but that wasn't his priority now. She was. "That's not why I'm here."

There was silence from the other side of the door; then she finally said, "It's not?"

He exhaled heavily, lifting his head but not his hand. "*Nay*. I'm just here to check on you." His voice cracked, and he took a moment to collect himself. "Because I love you, Lissie. Always have, always will. And if you don't want to marry me, I'll accept that."

"You will?"

Lissie rested her head and one hand against the door. Menno felt so close, yet miles away as she grappled with a mix of emotions. This was not at all what she had expected Menno to say. She thought he would argue with her, maybe even shout. Hearing him raise his voice might have been easier than hearing the gentle tone on the other side of the door. He said he wasn't here to argue, and she realized that was true because this wasn't his arguing voice.

He's here to make sure I'm oll recht.

A tear trickled down her cheek. She placed her hand on the doorknob, took a shuddering breath and turned the lock. She half expected him to yank the door open, but the knob didn't turn.

There was a moment of silence before Menno said, "Will you come outside? I know you're exhausted. I won't keep you long."

She opened the door and gazed up at Menno. The sight of him brought tears to her eyes again. "I'm okay," she told him. He backed up, and she stepped onto the porch, closing the door behind her.

"Wanna sit down?" He indicated the chairs where they'd spent many evenings discussing the life they would spend together.

Hugging herself, she shook her head no.

He glanced away, then back at her. "I'm sad you don't want to marry me, but…" He closed his eyes, then opened them. "But if you don't want to marry, don't love me the way I love you, then I agree, it's best we not wed."

His words made her breath catch in her throat and she fought not to dissolve into a sobbing mess. "It's not that, Menno," she choked. "It's not that I don't love you."

He clutched his hand to his chest. "Thank *Gott.* Because I don't know…if I could—" He gazed toward the little house he was supposed to vacate in the morning to live here in the big house with her. He stared into the darkness. "I don't know how I would live knowing you didn't love me. That you never—" He exhaled and shifted his gaze back to her. "You didn't plan this, did you?"

She drew back. "Plan *what*?"

He opened his arms wide. "The whole thing. Coming to Faith's Run, beginning our relationship anew. Making me so happy that nothing short of waking up to your beautiful face every morning would be enough. Agreeing to marry me and then walking out on me at the last moment." He drew his hand across his mouth. "Like I did to you. You know, to get even."

"To get *even*?" She rushed to him, grabbing both his hands. "Of course I'm not trying to get even with you, Menno. How could I? I didn't even know you had returned to Faith's Run. Not until you showed up at that bus stop in Dover three months ago." She studied his face, trying not to feel hurt that he would think she could do such a thing. "You didn't believe I could be so scheming, do you? What would make you think such a thing? Surely you know me better than that."

He squeezed her hands. "I do know you better. It's just that I was so shocked when you said you wouldn't marry me, I guess I lost my head for a few minutes. I was grasping in the dark for an explanation. It was Jude who set me straight."

She couldn't help but laugh. "Jude? Your brother, who's never had a second date in his life, was giving you advice?"

He smiled. "I know. I was surprised, too." He let go of her hand and pointed to the chairs. "Can we sit? All of a sudden, I'm dead on my feet. You must be, too."

She pushed back a lock of hair that had fallen from

beneath her prayer *kapp*. She was missing a hairpin from the organza head covering. "*Ya*, I'm tired."

They took the new Adirondack chairs positioned side by side with a small attached table between them. Both were silent. Lissie felt ashamed for having run off the way she did.

She glanced at him. The moon had risen in the dark sky, and its silvery light illuminated his face. Seeing him in that light, in Gott's light, softened her heart. "I'm sorry I took off like that. It was childish of me." Looking down, she twisted her hands in her lap. "I owe you an explanation."

"Lissie, you can always talk to me about anything."

She covered her face with her hand. "I was sitting under the maple tree watching the game and was suddenly overwhelmed by the idea of marrying you tomorrow. By the thought that we would be bound together for the rest of our lives when I wed you."

"And you aren't sure you want that with me?"

"No, oh no, Menno. It's not that at all," she gushed, turning in her chair to face him, their knees touching. "It's not you I'm not sure about. I love you. I love who you are to me, my children, your Daisy, your family, our church and community. It's me. I'm worried about me." When she rested her hand on the table between them, he covered it with his.

"Worried how?"

She squeezed her eyes shut. "The day that car hit you, it scared me so badly. I couldn't imagine living without you again and told you I'd marry you. But I said it on impulse."

"Okey." He drew the word out, obviously not sure what she meant. "Could you tell me more about that?"

She sighed. "I'm afraid impulsively agreeing to marry

you was a mistake. Like my impulsive decision to marry Alvan." The words came out in a rush. "And I wasn't the only one miserable in that marriage. Alvan was, too. I made him miserable because I wasn't the right woman for him. And then I brought children into the world and—" She couldn't finish that thought because it hurt too much to know she had been responsible for Naomi and Jonah's unhappy life in Ohio. "Menno, I was afraid—*am* afraid to marry you on impulse and regret it. Worse, for you to regret it."

"Oh, Lissie," he breathed, taking her hand between his. "These aren't the same circumstances as your marriage to Alvan."

"Nay?" she whispered.

He shook his head, smiling at her. "You may have been impulsive that day in the parking lot, but you and I had been talking about the possibility of marriage for weeks. And what about the years we talked about it before I left?"

His words surprised her. She hadn't seen it that way before.

"You didn't know Alvan, but you know me. And I know you. And yes, we've changed in some ways, but we're still the same people who long ago pledged our love to each other." He looked into her eyes. "I still love you. And you love me. And we belong together as husband and wife. Don't you think?" His last words sounded hopeful.

And he was right. Everything he had said was right. She did love him and she did want to be his wife. She looked out over the barnyard, barely able to make out the windmill that clicked as it spun in the evening breeze. "I'm so sorry, Menno. I was just so overwhelmed and scared." She looked back at him. "But I should have come to you and told you what I was feeling, not run away."

"I understand you being fearful after what you went through with Alvan. And I'm sorry for pushing you so hard about marrying. That was unfair. We don't have to get married now, we don't even have to get married this year. I'll wait for you, Lissie. I'll wait another ten years, if that's what you want." He rose, taking her hand and guiding her until they stood face-to-face. "I love you and I'll wait a lifetime for you."

She gazed up at him, smiling. "*Ach*, Menno." She brushed the blond hair off his forehead. "*Danki* for saying that."

"And thank you for giving me hope." He smiled down at her. "Now you should go to bed and I should return to *Mam*'s. I'll speak to the bishop first thing in the morning and get the word out to everyone that we're postponing. Indefinitely."

As Lissie gazed into his eyes, her heart swelled with joy. Suddenly she wasn't afraid anymore. "No need," she murmured.

"*Nay*, you should stay here and rest. You don't have to speak to anyone. I'll do it."

She stepped toward him and boldly rested her hands on his shoulders. "I mean, you'll not need to see Bishop Hamul."

He looked confused. "We don't want him showing up tomorrow morning thinking—"

"No need to tell him not to come," she interrupted, never more sure of herself than she was right now, "because we'll need him in the morning. When I marry you, Menno."

He froze. "Wait… What? You mean—"

"I'm saying I *want* to marry you, Menno," she whispered, meaning it with every fiber of her being. And now she wasn't afraid anymore. "It's all I've ever wanted."

"Oh, Lissie," he breathed.

He closed his eyes, leaning in to kiss her forehead, but she lifted her chin, and their lips met in their first kiss in over a decade. It was the sweetest kiss they had ever shared, one that promised a lifetime of love.

Epilogue

One Year Later

"I can't believe we're breaking in here in the dark," Lissie whispered with a giggle. "The children are going to be upset when they find out."

"Only if we tell them. They're catching fireflies in *Mam*'s yard. I doubt they've even noticed we're gone." Menno turned the key in the knob. He grabbed her hand and pulled her through the back door of the ice cream shop. "And it's not breaking in when you own the place."

She laughed lightheartedly. Since their wedding nearly a year ago, she had laughed every day like this. Life was so good with Menno and their children that sometimes she felt she needed to pinch herself to see if she was dreaming. By marrying Menno, her life and her children's lives had changed instantly, and all those changes were positive.

"It still doesn't feel seemly," she told him as they went through the doorway into an area where the ice cream freezers hummed. "Who sneaks out for ice cream without their children?"

"We do." He flipped a switch on the wall, casting just enough light to illuminate the work area where their employers scooped ice cream for customers before passing it through the service window. "You're the one who said she wanted mint chocolate chip ice cream in a waffle cone."

She tucked her hands behind her back. Barefoot, she wore one of the favorite blue dresses Sheba had made for her. Lissie giggled again for absolutely no reason other than sheer happiness. Most days were filled with activities that adults with children typically engaged in. They worked at their jobs, were active community members, maintained their home, and cared for their livestock and property. But Menno was great at capturing moments like this, making her feel like a teenager again, experiencing the thrill of new love.

Menno picked up an ice cream scoop and opened the sliding glass door to one of the chest freezers. "Still want mint chip?"

She pressed her hand to his back and peered in, enjoying the cold air that rose on the hot August evening. *"Ya."*

"One scoop?"

"Two," she said.

He turned his head to look at her, raising one eyebrow. "You never get two scoops. You're always about moderation."

Her gaze fell on the canisters of brightly colored candy sprinkles on the counter. "And sprinkles." She nibbled on her lower lip. "And maybe some chocolate chips." She looked around. "Is there whipped cream in the fridge?"

He took a waffle cone from a glass container and began to scoop out the ice cream. "There should be."

Standing beside him, she peered into the freezer again, watching him. Just seeing the frozen confection made her mouth water. "Maybe three scoops," she murmured.

He looked at her as if she had lost her mind, but added the extra dip. "Who are you? This is the second time you've said you were craving ice cream in the last three days." He passed her the cone and grabbed one for himself. "I think I'll have one scoop of chocolate, one of strawberry and one—" He stood up suddenly and looked at her. "Lissie?"

She took a lick of ice cream, delighting in the sweet, minty, chocolatey taste, and gazed at him over the edge of the big waffle cone. She heard the tone of his voice. He was on to her, but she feigned innocence. *"Ya?"*

"Are you… Could you be…"

She raised her eyebrows, trying hard not to break into a wide grin. She'd been planning to tell him her news all week, but she just hadn't had the chance. "Am I what?" she asked, having fun teasing him now.

"Are you…" He set his cone and the scoop down and turned to her.

She took another lick of the ice cream and held it out, struggling not to burst into joyous laughter. She had prayed for this for years, yet she still couldn't believe her prayers had been answered, with an abundance she hadn't thought possible. "Wanna taste? It's good. It'll be even better with sprinkles and whipped cream. Maybe a cherry."

He narrowed his gaze, appearing unsure of himself, which was unlike him, making her grin despite herself. "Is there something you need to tell me?"

"I already told you that the ice cream's delicious. The changes to your recipe are spot on."

He leaned toward her until their noses nearly touched over her ice cream cone. "You've been craving my ice cream. And you've slept in twice this week," he said softly. "Are you… Are we going to have a baby?"

Tears suddenly welled in her eyes. She couldn't stand it any longer. She had to tell him. "We are," she whispered.

He grabbed the cone from her hand, dropped it into a holder made for that purpose and wrapped his arms around her. "Oh, Lissie." Tears glistened in her beautiful blue eyes as he gazed at her. "I'd hoped…prayed *Gott* would bless us with children one day, but—" He didn't finish his sentence. Instead, he wrapped his arms more tightly around her, and she rested her head on his broad chest. "You've made me so happy," he whispered in her ear. "Who would have thought that running hand in hand through the woods all those years ago would bring us to this. Here. Now?"

She leaned back to gaze at his handsome face. "*Gott* did, Menno. It was all in His plan. I know that for certain."

He nodded and then lowered his head until his lips brushed hers, and Lissie knew she would be cherished and loved by this man for all the days of her life.

* * * * *

Dear Reader,

I hope you enjoyed your first visit to the Amish community of Faith's Run in Kent County, Delaware. The moment I "met" Elizabeth Bontrager and her family, I knew her boys each deserved their own book. Her eldest son, Menno, seemed the perfect place to start. While it's difficult to find exact numbers, approximately 10-15% of young Amish men and women leave their communities. There's even less data on how many return later, but it happens occasionally. When creating Menno and Lissie's story, I asked myself why a young man would return, and the answer came quickly. Folks like Menno return to Amish society for the life of faith, community and family. And even though Lissie hadn't left the church, strong community and family ties brought her back to Faith's Run.

I don't know about you, but I was relieved when Lissie and Menno managed to find their way back to each other. So often we don't understand life's twists and turns, but God always has a plan for us, doesn't He?

Now that Menno, Lissie, and their children are settled, I should start thinking about Jude Bontrager. He's never had much success dating, but he wants a wife and family, and I have a feeling that wish will come true. The question is, how will his story unfold?

Blessings,
Emma Miller